H. Baden (Henry Baden) Pritchard

Tramps In The Tyrol

H. Baden (Henry Baden) Pritchard

Tramps In The Tyrol

ISBN/EAN: 9783741149375

Manufactured in Europe, USA, Canada, Australia, Japa

Cover: Foto ©Andreas Hilbeck / pixelio.de

Manufactured and distributed by brebook publishing software (www.brebook.com)

H. Baden (Henry Baden) Pritchard

Tramps In The Tyrol

TRAMPS IN THE TYROL.

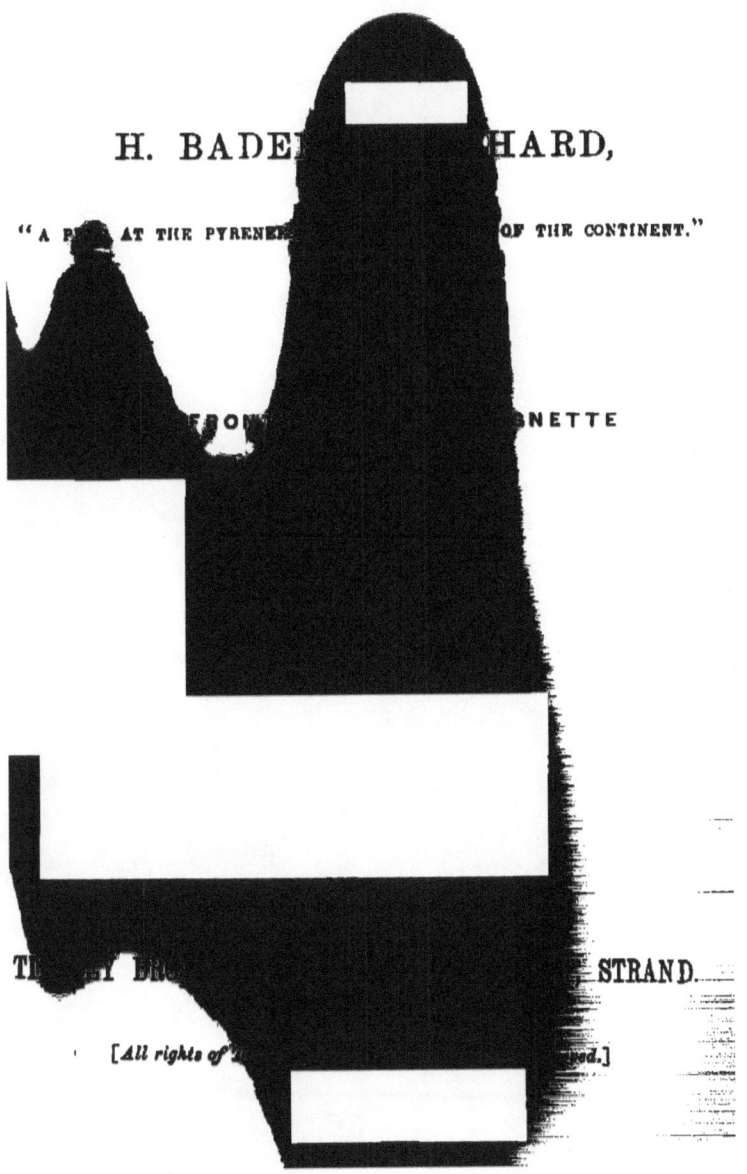

H. BADE   HARD,

"A ... AT THE PYRENE ... OF THE CONTINENT."

... NETTE

... STRAND.

CONTENTS.

CHAPTER I.

CHAPTER II.

CHAPTER III.

CHAPTER IV.

CHAPTER V.

CHAPTER VI.

CHAPTER VII.

CHAPTER VIII.

CHAPTER IX.

CHAPTER X.

CHAPTER XI.

INTRODUCTION.

A FEW words regarding the compilation of this volume are perhaps necessary. Where all have contributed so equally, it is invidious to refer to individuals. Still, in all fairness, it must be stated that if any passages of sentiment are found to grace the pages, if any poetic feeling or pathos should be discovered, the same are solely and entirely due to Green's quill, and, it may be added, are copyright. The daring adventures and hairbreadth escapes were all undertaken by White, whose only privilege it was to encounter them ;* while Black's

---

* These being strictly personal and somewhat uninteresting, have been omitted.

quarto diary and Brown's note-book have furnished details of the route and other matters.

It may be argued by critics that there is a certain uneven and irregular style to be found throughout the work; but this, it must be pointed out, is just the feature of the book—the gist of the whole thing, in fact. Several minds cannot be engaged upon a task without some impress of them remaining behind; and this naturally accounts for the variation, or, as some might call it, limping style, of composition which the reader may take, perhaps, for bad writing.

THE TITTLEBAT CLUB,
    WATER LANE, E.C.

TRAMPS IN THE TYROL.

CHAPTER I.

BASLE—LAKE OF CONSTANCE—LINDAU—THE ORIGINATOR OF
THE TOUR—IMMENSTADT—PLEASURES OF PEDESTRIANS—
BEER-FEVER—AN OBSTREPEROUS KNAPSACK.

*R**EISEN sie ab?"*

" *Mais prenez vos billets !"*

· " *Vere you go to ?"*

It was the Basle railway station, and
Brown had hurried off for a moment to
purchase tickets for Lindau, leaving his
three companions at the mercy of half a
dozen excited porters. That there was
some reason for this bustle and hubbub, it
must be admitted. The pedestrians, knapsack on back, had performed a hasty march
through the town from one terminus to the

other; they arrived late; they managed to come in by a side entrance, and at the station, the authorities, besides speaking three languages, to suit further all sorts of travellers, accommodatingly keep three kinds of time—French, German, and Swiss. Frantic officials surrounded the Englishmen on all sides, and Brown only effected his escape after some difficulty. The clerk who sold the tickets, or rather his legs, were quickly found, but the way to get into the office, short of diving under a partition that screened the man's body, was the exasperating problem. From one door to another did Brown rush, only to find room after room filled with gruff silver-laced officials, and things were coming to a pass, when chance suddenly brought the pay place into view. But in the meanwhile Green, anxious to aid his leader, had dived under the vexatious partition, so that when

Brown, in a perspiration, was seeking to purchase tickets in front, the man's nether limbs were being excitedly attacked by Green in the rear. The main party the while, being weakened by loss of numbers, were in a fair way of being worried to death by contending nationalities, and poor Black and White were not rescued by their friends a moment too soon. A rush was made for the carriages, the Britons succeeded in the assault, and then the station was formally closed to the public—a ceremony performed by a tall, bearded official, who solemnly shut the middle of three big open doors.

After the storm came a calm. To the wild scene of excitement succeeded a quiet journey of a dozen hours, and the leisurely motion of the train came as a welcome relief. The frequent stoppages at the rustic stations allowed plenty of time for soothing

the feelings, as well as studying the manners and customs of Helvetia, the train
making its way in a most deliberate, easy-
going manner. The line of railway, too,
seemed to be under no restraint, for it
meandered about just where its own sweet
will pleased. It left Switzerland for a time
and passed into the Duchy of Baden, and
presently came back again among the mountains. Anon it followed the Rhine, when
there was anything of interest to be seen,
like the grand Falls of Schaffhausen, and
then again it lost itself among fir-clad hills,
until it turned up once more at the Lake of
Constance, where passengers to Lindau and
Germany take boat and exchange the pleasant railway for the still more pleasant
steamer. lying close by with its steam up
ready to start.

The day is very hot, and the placid water
invitingly suggests coolness and repose.

There is not a ripple nor a breath of air; the lake is one glassy expanse, and as the prow cuts its way sharply through the limpid blue water, it scatters liquid gems along its path. The passengers sit listlessly under the awning, or recline at full length in the sun upon the packages strewn about the deck. The scene is one of dreamy inactivity. Scarcely a sound is heard beyond the noise of the engines, for no one cares to exert himself so far as to open his lips, save, perhaps, when something of particular interest calls for attention. The crew move lazily to and fro; the captain from the bridge contemplates vacantly the soft hazy banks on either side, and the look-out is fast asleep at the prow. The cook prepares dinner with the air of a martyr, and passes through a fiery ordeal in the galley to very little purpose. A more fitting place or season for a noonday's siesta it would be difficult to suggest; even the paddles seem to take up the idea, for after a time they too beat lazily and with greater deliberation.

In due time the steamer makes the pretty harbour of Lindau, where, after a brief rest, railway travelling is resumed for a couple of hours. This is the Fatherland at last, and the lofty blue outlines in front are the outposts of the Tyrol. Pine-clad hills and undulating pastures, fresh and green, succeed the views of lake and mountain as the pedestrians approach their destination.

And here it should be distinctly stated that it was Brown who was mainly instrumental in originating the journey about to be described. This much must be clearly understood at the outset, so that when the historical value of these records comes to be fully appreciated hereafter, and their merit universally acknowledged, there shall be no question at all as to the master mind in whose brain the idea germinated. This preliminary announcement is of the utmost importance, as all who have any knowledge of pedestrian tours will at once admit, for when marching in company, too much stress cannot be laid upon the matter of priority, and each individual traveller is bound to assert his claim stoutly and defiantly to any discovery or idea he thinks he has made. For instance, if Green discovers a distant glacier or an old church spire some two minutes before the rest, it would be a nice thing indeed were friend Black or White afterwards to lay claim to having seen them first ; or where a short cut has been found to be more than usually out of the way, surely the first to find out its roundaboutedness has a right to say that from the very outset he was confident the path taken was wrong. Without the development of this element of positiveness, or more correctly speaking "cocksuredom," no party of pedestrian tourists could hang together for a single day, for the principal cause of bickerings and disputes would be wanting; and in the present case it may be safely affirmed that it was only by reason of such constant interchange of personal opinion, that the companions felt an interest in sticking together at all, and journeying in company.

It was Brown then who, after urgent solicitations from several members, suggested one evening at the Tittlebat Club the making up of a party to walk round the Gross Glockner.

"The Gross what?" had Green asked eagerly, being the only one not above showing his ignorance.

"The Gross Glockner," Brown returned.

"Oh, that?" said Green. "Oh yes, of course; I thought you said somewhere else."

And in this way it was settled off-hand to go into the Gross Glockner district, but where the Gross Glockner was, or of what the Gross Glockner consisted, none but the proposer had the faintest idea.

"I suppose," ventured White, carefully angling for information, "you'll go by Newhaven and Dieppe?"

"And stop a night at Rouen; that's what we did when we went to the Pyrenees, you know," added Black.

"Certainly not," replied Brown; "why, that would be losing no end of time."

White merely said, "Ah! yes, so it would;" and no more suggestions were made. Green, however, distinguished himself once more. "Could the thing with the strange name be up somewhere in Norway?" he thought. So he ventured in an off-hand manner, "I should say it would be best to go there direct by boat."

Brown was in amazement. "By boat! Why, man, what on earth do you mean?"

And White and Black could contain their merriment no longer, but laughed to tears at the idea of Green wanting to go all the way to the Gross Glockner by steamer.

"Why, the Gross Glockner is one of the highest peaks in the Tyrol, in the midst of mountains and glaciers," was Brown's remark.

"Why, it's hundreds of miles inland," said White.

"The idea of going there by sea is what I like!" gasped Black. And it was some time before these two were able to cease laughing at Green's mishap—the joke was really such a good one.

*   *   *   *   *

At last the railway journey is brought to an end, and Immenstadt is reached, the point at which the knapsacks are to be donned and walking to commence. The train is quitted with a sense of relief, and all feel that the time has come for beginning the march in real earnest. That strapping on of the knapsacks . and assumption of blouses is a serious affair, by no means to be regarded with levity, while the adjusting of buckles, the slinging round of flasks, and the looking to belts and other paraphernalia are matters of immense consideration : and very important and determined doth the Tittlebat Club appear in their walking equipment : if only their friends at home could have beheld them, the triumph would be complete, for the few lookers-on at the station fail perhaps to be impressed with the proper amount of admiration, and wonder, no doubt, what it all means.

" All ready, now ?" calls Brown, in a sten-torian voice.

Just another tightening of a strap, and

the taking-in of another hole in a belt, and the tying-up of a bootlace, and the screwing-up of a flask-stopper (with all due care, caution, and solemnity of course), and the travellers stand ready for the road.

"All ready, now?" demands Brown, for a second time; and then, with shoulders squared and heads erect, the party march off abreast through the little town.

The start can scarcely be called a fair one though, for at the very outset White leads the line by mistake right down a bye-lane that leads nowhere : and the entrance being at once barred by wondering natives, who followed, curious to find out what the travellers wanted to go down there for, there is no alternative but to scramble ignominiously in single file past a row of pigsties, and so into the main road again.

Barring this little mishap, however

(which Brown, by the way, was quite certain would happen, when he saw White lead off), there is nothing to stop the martial progress, or check the advance of the explorers towards the Tyrol. Was there ever such a glorious sight as these stalwart Britons on their way to do battle with the mountains? Did the simple folk of Immenstadt ever witness before so bold and determined an undertaking? Did they ever see such sturdy pedestrians led by so stalwart a mountaineer? So thinks White, as he strides on valiantly half a pace in advance, and with a swing too that seems untiring. Head thrown proudly back, nostrils dilated, and lips pursed up, there can be no doubt about his prowess and staying qualities, even if these were not confirmed by an occasional shake or toss of the head very knowing and solemn to behold. He certainly has a jaunty, devil-

may-care sort of air about him, has White,
quite awe-inspiring to see.   And as he
glances with dignity to each side of the
road, his looks seem to say benignantly,
" Ye good people of Immenstadt" (apostrophizing two little girls dabbling in the
town fountain), " Ye good people of Immenstadt, who are bred and born here, you may,
of course, see and admire the mountains as
much as you will, but it is left to brave
and   energetic   Britons — Tittlebatonians
and the like—to scale and put them under
their feet.   Fear not for us, good people of
Immenstadt, we shall come to no harm,
although we are going to do wonderful and
dangerous things ; even those hazy mountains you see in the distance yonder will
not confine us ; no, we are going on right
past them—on, on, on, until we come to
the regions of snow and ice.   Good-bye,
good people, and God bless you.   We have

no objection to your cheering and throwing up your caps, for we really are wonderful fellows; and, although we don't actually tell you so, still you can see it by our look, and the manner in which we sway about as we march along."

Hurrah for the knapsack! Who so cheery and so light-hearted as the pedestrian as he steps along a pretty lane between green hedgerows, or climbs a bit of mountain road, and watches the village pictures in the valley below? who so independent and happy, when needing a quiet rest he throws off his burden, and reclines upon some soft slope, or in the deep shadow of the walnut-trees that border the path? Who so careless and free in his actions? the light weight he carries is surely no burden; and stories and anecdotes and songs enliven the way, when there are no natural beauties to admire. Who so fresh, so joyous, and so chatty—especially at the start? It is singular though, that after a few miles there is scarcely so much talking and singing as at first; and the marching, perhaps, is a little less like a pendulum movement. A weak point here, or a slight pain there, develops itself, but you are not tired for all that. Not at all: on you go, mile after mile, rather silent, and puffing and blowing a little, it is true, but footsore and weary! —why, who ever heard of such a thing?

There is nothing to fear and nothing to care for, to speak of, saving—in warm weather, mind you—one particular ailment; a failing, in fact, which is as prevalent among pedestrians as it is among German students. It is a singular sickness, known under the name of *Bier-durst*, or beer-fever; and a word respecting it will not be out of place here. The disease is peculiar to the Fatherland. In no other country do you

experience it. A burning thirst gradually
dries up all the available bodily moisture.
This thirst will not be cured with water.
It cries out distinctly for beer! beer! and
one of its worst symptoms is that the patient
passes into a state of great irritation if the
beer is drawn with too much head. The
first mug is swallowed without any effect,
and the second is ordered with the injunction
to the doctor—that is, the beer maiden—
"*Liebes Mädchen, nur nicht zu viel Schaum.*"
Should the second dose fail to give instant
relief, a third will be found an unfailing
remedy, so that the ailment is not after all
a very serious one, if only promptly and
properly treated.

"Nine miles done, and here we are in
sight of Hinterlangen; very good marching,
capital!" exclaims Brown.

White is no longer half a pace ahead of
the line; he evidently has thought better of

2

it, and come to the conclusion that it looks
bad for any one to be so far in advance of
the others, and so, for modesty's sake, he
has dropped back ; nay, his absence of pride
is such that he prefers to be rather behind
than in advance of his comrades.

"A most singular feeling," he presently
remarks, pulling up short after two or three
ineffectual spurts to get up.   "A most singular feeling, do you know, under my arm,
as if one of the straps were giving way !   I
should just like to see if it really is the case."

Green, dear good fellow that he is, volunteers to look.   With the greatest alacrity he
throws off his own dusty knapsack and
stretches his arms leisurely, as a preliminary to the inspection.

"A great nuisance, having to pull up,"
says Brown, but nevertheless he too is a good
fellow, and don't object to wait a few moments, lying down meanwhile at full length

on the cool grass with the best grace possible.

A great deal of pulling and stretching and contriving is necessary before White's knapsack is all right again—Green, in order to assist the better, being obliged to lie on his back the while. There is nothing really important the matter, but you see White's shoulders are rather ill-suited to the knapsack, and somehow—one hardly knows how to express it—it pulls, or pushes, or does something or other which it ought not to do, in a most unaccountable manner. Very singular; not that the weight is in any way cumbersome or tiring, you know, but the straps are not exactly what they should be. White is a splendid walker, and of course not in the least fatigued, and it is so annoying, therefore, that the wretched leather should cut into his shoulders in this absurd fashion. Green's knapsack is

in capital order, luckily, not a fault to be
found with it, and he could go on, he intimates, for ages without stopping.   He never
was in better training too than at present,
and therefore, he explains, could sustain any
amount of fatigue.

The idea, indeed, of any one being tired,
after a mere nine-mile walk, is naturally
quite ridiculous, and all agree, as they stretch
themselves out comfortably upon the grass,
that they were never fresher or more
lively.

"I'll tell you what, though," said Green,
getting up into a sitting posture, "and this
too is rather singular.   My elbow-joint,
don't you know, that I hurt last year when
rowing; I just feel the pain again slightly.
It is not at all serious, but it is rather
strange that the pain should come on just
now."

This statement, Green volunteers merely

as a casual remark, and not of course in any way as a matter bearing upon present circumstances. He bares his elbow and shows it to White, who examines it with a doubtful shake of the head.

Presently Brown starts a proposition, which somehow comes quite unexpectedly upon everybody. " It would be well, perhaps, to stop the night at Hinterlangen and go no further till next morning." Nothing was so bad, he argued, as over-exertion at the first start off.

Black's experience in the Pyrenees confirmed this view of affairs, but White and Green rather demurred to the proposal; they were both so exquisitely fresh, and so eager for a good stiff march, that it would be a serious disappointment not to go any further. However, on second thoughts, it would probably be best, after all, they agreed, provided they started ever so early next morning for a right down good walk and no nonsense about it.

And so in quite a jovial mood all get briskly on their legs again, and step along the short distance of road that separates them from the village.

CHAPTER II.

THERE may be finer country elsewhere
than that about Hinterlangen, but a
more smiling and prosperous district it
would be difficult to find. Not only are
the cottages and homesteads large and
well-built, but there pervades an air of
cleanliness and comfort rarely met with in
mountain villages. Carefully-tended flower-
gardens gladden the eye at every turn, and
over the trimly-kept cottages are trained
all kinds of creepers and shrubs suggestive
of sweet odours and cool shade. Gaily-
painted frescoes are seen upon the shining
white walls, and clinging around the

porches are roses and jasmine bines in full
blossom. The highly cultivated land pro-
claims the presence of well-to-do farmers ;
and the numerous inns in the valley seem
to tell of their jollity and good living.

It was at the sign of the Eagle that
the Tittlebatonians established themselves,
and very well merited was the patronage
bestowed. The last Englishman who had
signed the visitors' book had been gone
nearly a year ; and judging from his description in that volume—he was put down
as a "privateer" by some student of the
English language—the host was well rid
of him. Green hazarded an opinion that
this might account for the lack of spoons in
the salt-cellars ; but the fallacy of such a
conclusion was at once pointed out by
Brown, who explained that salt-spoons on
the Continent, like top-coats among the
Ashantees, are articles not in general use.

Of course so benighted a state of things
could not fail to be thoroughly discussed, and
White philanthropically suggested that on
the return of the party to the centre of
civilization, meaning London, measures
should be taken to establish a salt-spoon
missionary society to lecture upon the pur-
poses of this domestic instrument throughout the land. It is true, as a set-off, big
egg-cups were invariably used for drinking
coffee out of in this part of the world ; but
as Green most cogently remarked, it is difficult to see what this has to do with the
spoon question.

From Hinterlangen the road steeply inclines through a dark pine forest, and the
view back at the pretty pastoral valley is
one that will linger long in the traveller's
memory. The crucifixes and little white
chapels so frequently met with harmonize
well with the landscape, and seem, for the

most part, to have been planted with a
great deal of forethought. An eminence
which affords a good look-out, a turn in
the road when a new scene bursts into view,
the top of a steep ascent when one is in
need of rest, are the spots chosen for the
erection of these emblems of religion. Crucifixes, or niches in the rock, containing
some religious picture, are the most frequent; but occasionally, at every mile or two
there are little wayside chapels, affording
room for a dozen or more worshippers; and
these are sometimes fitted-up with much
rustic taste. Such a one is passed on the
way to Oberdorf, offering the traveller
friendly shelter from the weather. And it
is with feelings of disgust that one sees the
tiny walls covered with the names of brag-
gart busybodies (thank goodness, none
were English), who, not content with
scrawling their dirty autographs over the

altar, had finished up by forcing the poor-box.

It is difficult to say why the sign-post at Oberdorf reminds one, all at once, of " Little Billee ;" but probably because the information it gives is so very general. "To the Tyrol," it says, comprehensively pointing up a bye-lane to a country twice as big as Switzerland. Then which is the way to "North and South Amerikee," and to "Jerusalem and Madagascar ?" and whereabouts is Japan and Timbuctoo? one wants to know. If you once begin with generalities, there seems to be no stopping. However, if you have made up your mind to go to the Tyrol, you must take care to follow straight along the turning pointed out; where the other path, that leads over a gate and across a small turnip field, goes to—goodness only knows ! But, by the way, it is scarcely just, fter all, to qauarrel with the sign-post

for there are very few of them to be found,
and as in the present case it tells all one
wants to know, what more ,can be desired ?
So on past Oberdorf, and past the last Bava-
rian turnpike, differing from other turnpikes
in the fact that the keeper can lift up or
pull down the bar without getting out of
his warm bed—an arrangement deserving
the notice of all easy-going toll-keepers.

To go all the way to Austria thirty-six
times running, within five minutes, is certainly quick travelling, but White, for the
sole benefit of Mrs. White, who was to be
acquainted with the fact in the first letter,
accomplished the journeys well within that
time ; and any well-meaning friend who
may inadvertently ask the distinguished
traveller on his return whether he has ever
been within the Austrian dominions, is to
be pitied.   If he manages to stem the flood
of indignation with which he will be en-

countered, he will be a sensible man, as much so perhaps as the Austrian customs' officer who wished to examine the knapsacks of the party on the frontier. This worthy official insisted that all the little packages should be opened one by one, and their contents minutely examined before proceeding further; and simply because his wishes were attended to in every particular, he chose to believe that a joke was being played upon him. Nothing must do but that every packet should be opened and a formal inspection made; and so it was unanimously decided that the officer should have his own way, although not exactly his own way of having it. As if Britons were going to let him rummage about in their knapsacks just as he pleased! this would never do, so his advances were firmly repelled, until the kits were all of them properly ordered for general inspection, and every

article had been emptied out and systemati-
cally arranged upon the grassy slope in
military order. There was not very much
to look at, it must be confessed, all said and
done, and, besides, the linen and wearing
apparel exhibited were scarcely of a nature
to be proud of. Nevertheless, the service-
able old stockings and tumbled night-shirts
were folded with due care and precision;
slippers placed properly right and left, and
the extra pair of inexpressibles laid at full
length to show there was no deception.
Soap, razor, and brush were shown, as were
also two little fronts and roll of collars.
Unfortunately, before the complete arrangement of the articles could be effected to the
entire satisfaction of the party, the repre-
sentative of the Austrian empire got tired
of such elaborate preparations, and retired
within his stronghold in great dudgeon;
and he could, under no circumstances, be pre-

vailed upon to come out again to make the inspection in the proper official manner. The time and trouble incurred in these preliminary measures were therefore thrown away, and after waiting a considerable time upon the railings opposite for the gentleman in uniform, the club formally resolved that it was useless to delay any longer, and so proceeded carefully to repack their property and to continue their journey.

The pancakes and salad, which composed the dinner at Nesselwangen, would have been passed over without comment, only a deep-set scheme on the part of Green and White deserves mention, a dodge noteworthy on the score of its ingenuity alone. To prevent too heavy payment being demanded, from the host supposing his guests to be English, the proposition was whispered, "Why not pretend to be Dutch?" and in support of this idea, the gentlemen above

named conceived the clever notion of singing
snatches of "Meynheer Van Dunck" throughout the banquet, to impress the waitress,
who had never probably been beyond her
native village, with a belief of their Low
Land nationality. And here just another
word on the subject of beer drinking, for
this beverage is so good hereabouts that
one may feel tempted to indulge too much
therein. "You should never," said the host,
in measured terms and with the air of one
who spoke from dearly-bought experience,
"you should never drink off a glass of beer
after a walk, without taking a little *Schnapps*
first of all." This was a mistake which
many people committed, so a medical man
had told him, and he had never forgotten the
warning. Always take a little drop of something short before drinking beer, or, if yon
can't do that—well, cough deliberately three
times, and the effect will be just the same.

And so through the pretty Gacht Pass, with its sombre green slopes and broad meadow land, where the wild blossoms in the fields are so bright and plentiful that at times one is walking almost breast-high in a gay parterre of flowers ; down steep winding terraces that afford charming prospects at every turn, and along mountain paths with frowning black ravines below, so wild and precipitous as to impart a fearful fascination to the giddy and nervous, and then on by smiling white villages, homely and pic-turesque. The valley gradually broadens, and the rapid torrent changes to a brawling river as you come in sight of Reutte, a little market town at the junction of several valleys.

From Reutte to Lermos, a dozen miles or so, the diligence, or Eilwagen, is taken for the double purpose of affording a rest and accelerating the journey, for Innsbrück and the Glockner district still lies many miles in front. Places are booked at the post-office, and the way-bill, or rather receipt, made out with due deliberation and serious-ness by the spectacled postmaster. The big lumbering vehicle only carries three passengers, and as the interior is already occupied by its complement of two, there is but one place left in the coupé beside the conductor. This Brown volunteered to take, while the other three were carefully wedged into a supplementary coach by the guard, who was very solicitous indeed that they should be firmly fixed therein, lest any accident occur from the severe jolting and shaking experienced over the moun-tain roads.

The guard enjoyed Brown's company immensely, as also his cigars and the con-tents of his flask. He had no idea that the party behind had any connexion with his companion in the coupé, and on one of the frequent halts, during which the carriage in rear had been carefully inspected, he came back laughing so immoderately that Brown demanded to be a sharer of the merriment. But it was only after great difficulty that the cause of it could be made clear, and the guard literally choked with laughter as he endeavoured to explain, in short gasps, what it was all about.

"They are a comical folk truly, those English—*ein komisches Volk, wahrhaftig, ein komisches Volk*—they tell me they are on a pleasure excursion, and they spend all day in trudging up and down the mountains."

Brown agreed that it was a funny thing certainly, but then an Englishman's eccentricity was proverbial.

"I'll tell you such a good story," said the guard, when with his eyes full of tears he had coughed himself quiet into a corner of the coupé. "An Englishman came down here last year, *komischer Kerl* he was truly, and wanted to go fishing in the lake at Hesterang. So away he went to the fish-master who rents the water about here, and asked how much must be paid for permission. Well," continued the guard, his voice commencing to shake again with another fit of laughter that was coming on; " well, the fish-master, of course, thinking the Englishman was only joking, told him that for a florin a day he might do as he liked. Would you believe it; every day, for more than a month actually, the Englishman worked hard from morn till night catching fish, and, as I live"—here the guard fairly broke out again—"as I live, instead of keeping the fish that he caught for himself, he used to come regularly and give them up; so the end of it was, that the fish-master lay in bed the whole day,

while the Englishman not only went out
fishing for him, but actually paid a lot of
florins for being allowed to do the work.
Ah! they are *komisches Volk* truly, those
Englishmen."

Brown laughed as much over the joke as
ever his informant did, and this so encou-
raged the guard that he launched forth into
another story, which he prefaced, however,
with the remark, that he could not actually
vouch for its accuracy, as he only knew of
it by hearsay. The story was something as
follows :—

An Englishman, it appears, went to an
hotel in Innsbrück. It is well to note, by
the way, that most comic stories told by the
natives of Switzerland and its neighbourhood
begin with the words "an Englishman,"
and this of itself is so invariably considered
the sure sign of a good story that listeners
at once make ready to hear something

funny. An, Englishman went to an hotel
in Innsbrück, and on leaving was presented
with a bill amounting to thirty-six kreuzers
(nothing is said about the florins), and this
he refused to pay on the ground that it was
excessive. "But you must pay it," said
the host; "the train for Munich starts in
half an hour, and your luggage shan't
leave my house."

"Don't care, *alles nichts, alles nichts !*"
said the Englishman, in a temper, sweeping his arm from right to left in good
bold Briton style; "I wont pay thirty-six
kreuzers; I'll go to the magistrate."

"The train will leave without you, if you
do," said the host.

"Don't care—*alles nichts !*" replied the
Englishman, repeating the sweeping action;
"*alles nichts*, I wont pay the thirty-six
kreuzers." And away he went to the magistrate, who decided in the Briton's favour,

and decreed that twenty-four kreuzers was
a sufficient sum to pay.

" Ah ! but you have lost your train," said
the host, as he received the reduced amount
with a grin.

" *Alles nichts,*" said the determined man,
more determined than ever; "send my
luggage to the railway."

But when he got to the station he was
informed that there was no train till the
morning. " Don't care, *alles nichts !*" still
pursued the obstinate Briton ; "put on a
special train directly, here's gold, here's
money enough," and with that he took out
a handful of Napoleons, and threw them
upon the counter.

The guard would no doubt have continued the recital of stories still more wonderful, in illustration of the well-known
obstinacy and wealth of Britons, had not
one of the party behind walked up—the

vehicles were going slowly up hill—and, conversing with Brown, unfortunately put an end to the fun; for the guard had little to say until they arrived at Lermos, when, on parting, he gave Brown his address, in case the latter, or any of his dear friends in England, might desire to purchase a tame chamois which the guard had for sale, and which he was willing to part with for a mere song—say a few Napoleons.

CHAPTER III.

LERMOS—POLITE SOCIETY—PRIMITIVE LODGINGS—THE MA-
RIENBURG—A CLUB MEETING—AN ACCIDENT—RULES
OF PEDESTRIANISM—POSTING—INNSBRÜCK.

BUT if the guard departed, he left behind
him at the inn, where the Eilwagen
stopped, one of the occupants of the interior, a Prussian lady of mature age, who
was good enough to be very kind and
gracious, because, so it afterwards turned out,
she had mistaken Anglo-Saxon for French;
believing the party to be some of her fallen
foes to whom it was but generous to show
clemency and forgiveness. The seductive
and engaging nature of this lady's conversation, directed from the head of the table
whence she superintended the Tittlebatonians
with winning politeness, was as unceasing

as it was rapid, the most charming super-
latives being thrown off in quick succession.

The *wunderschön* and *reizend* scenery of
the Tyrol was only equalled by the *allerliebst*
character of the inhabitants, to say nothing
of the *prachtrolles* weather just then. · The
Tyrol could not, of course, be compared to
Switzerland for some things, for there was
no Giessbach, no Lake of Geneva, and no
Jungfrau; the Black Forest was not, of
course, in Switzerland, but that was also
most charming, as likewise the Danube, and
the Elbe above Dresden; they called it
Saxon Switzerland, but she, for her part,
much preferred the district around Thuringia,
although, it was true, they spoke such out-
rageous German about there that one always
longed to get back to Hanover and Hamburg, where, by the way, the Prussian
garrison was making itself very agreeable, it was said, and several really nice

matches had already been made between the
young military noblemen and the best
Hamburg families; and it was whispered
too that some of the young lieutenants
there were more closely connected with the
Imperial Family at Berlin than one chose
to say, &c. &c.

During a pause in the conversation,
Brown came back again to more practical
matters, and discussing travelling in the
Tyrol, complained of the difficulty there
was occasionally of getting meat for dinner
at the little roadside inns.

" Oh, it is really too *fürchterlich,"* said
the lady with a shudder, unwinding another
skein of conversation; " it is really too
fearful. I am travelling for the very purpose
of re-establishing my health, and the food
sometimes set before you it is impossible to
eat. When the Eilwagen stopped for
dinner to-day there was a sort of sweet

syrupy mixture for soup that I could not
touch, then some fat veal fried in I don't
know what, a dish one could scarcely
look at; then a *Mehlspeise*, or pancake of
some kind, which the waitress regarded as
something quite superior, but which I could
not eat a mouthful of, while the conductor sat
near me all the time at the same table and
devoured everything with the greatest avidity.
As I told the waitress, really they should
leave off having such messes and substitute
some nice wholesome food, or some of the
dishes one gets at railway stations, or the
German beer gardens, or at the restaurants
in Hanover and Hamburg," where everything, the fair traveller averred, was *vornehm,*
elegant, and *delicat.*

Supper was got through in a very short
time that night, on account of the early
retirement of Brown and Black, who were
taken off by their friends in a state of giddy

excitement. While, on the one hand, these two gallants had been endeavouring to withstand the German fire and pay some attention to the speaker, they had, at the same time been badgered all through by Green, who, not being sufficiently acquainted with the Saxon tongue, importuned the two linguists to translate some ardent love passages made up by White and himself for the benefit of the German Fair.

The good people at the Post inn in Lermos have primitive ideas as to the entertainment of travellers. Like the guards on most Continental railways, who seem to have a pride in crowding their carriages, and for this reason completely fill some of the compartments, while others are locked up and kept empty, so the host or hostess here managed the sleeping accommodation. When bedtime came, and the party was ushered upstairs, the waitress, leading the

way, opened a door, and finding two beds
therein, out of four, disengaged, at once
detached two of the travellers to occupy
them, while the remaining two were put
into a treble-bedded room, having as yet
but one occupant. All this was done in a
straightforward, business-like manner, and
as there seemed to be no appeal, it only remained for the pedestrians to take matters
as they found them.

A pedestrian has the choice of two ways
in going to Miemingen on the road to Innsbrück, one by the post road, a most beautiful
route, and one by the Marienburg, which
goes over a pass some five thousand feet
high, and leads direct into the village of
Obersteig. Naturally enough, with such
mountaineers as White and Green, the road
was not to be thought of for a moment, but
the way over the Marienburg chosen by
reason of its greater difficulty. Were the

hardy climbers, at the first opportunity, to show the white feather, and forego the glory of shouting "Excelsior?" Perish the thought! away up the giddy height, to conquer or to die.

It was somewhat in this mood that they turned out of the high-road up a steep ascent clothed in pines, clambering the stony path with a freshness and vigour that lasted for fully ten minutes. In fact, the whole two hours' ascent would have been performed in the same spirit throughout had not that treacherous knapsack of White's again got out of order; the tiresome straps became tightened from some unaccountable cause every five minutes, and the only way of pressing them back into shape was for the wearer to lean the pack firmly against a tree every now and then, and to wait patiently until the contrivance left off hurting. It is needless to say that

under such trying circumstances the others,
to a man, sympathized sincerely with poor
White, and were indeed so cut up about the
dear fellow, that they could never look on
at his suffering except in a sitting posture.
And in this way they waited, without an
impatient word on their lips, until the victim
felt disposed to proceed, although Brown, it
must be admitted, grumbled a little at the
" demoralizing" effect of such delays; and
Black bore witness that such things never
occurred when he was in the Pyrenees.
Green took the matter in very good part, and
was even so kind as to propose taking a rest,
if White thought such a proceeding would
relieve him at all.   But to this the suffering
athlete, as he leaned against a big pine
trunk quietly smoking " half a pipe," would
not for a moment consent to; for, as he said
very truly, to make a creditable affair of it,
they ought to proceed as they were doing,

and march straight away to the summit without resting at all.

And the feat was performed, too, under the regulation time, deducting, of course, the hour and a half taken up by White's refractory straps. The village of Lermos, in the valley below, might have been co-vered with a wide-awake, so small did it appear, and the little lake by the side of the road was a tiny bit of looking-glass, let into a cavity among the black fir-trees. Hill tops seemed to spring up from everywhere, and there was not a flat stretch of ground to be seen on any side. Red Alpine roses and blue-eyed forget-me-nots decked the grassy mountain-sides, and formed a pretty fore-ground to the rugged peaks beyond.

This being the first grand ascent, a club meeting was at once called to celebrate the event, and to hear a proposition from the valiant White. "We must constitute ourselves a reporting staff, and write a book of travels for our friends," he suggested. The idea was received with tremendous acclamation, and carried *nem. con.* But a knotty argument cropped up as to the nature of this report. What should be its character? what kind of report was it to be? what would the friends like best? was the book to be a grand account of the whole journey, or merely a skeleton outline of the tour? was it to be a work of first-class order, or only of mediocre quality; or, as Green somewhat vulgarly put it, was the thing to be "duffin or good?" Green was of the idea that it would turn out "duffin" after all, but this notion was scouted at once, and by a majority it was declared that the account of the tour should be a decidedly clever production. Under these circumstances, of course, it is merely necessary to warn the reader to look out for good things, for the resolution, having once been passed, it cannot now be rescinded. And here, to enliven the next page, there shall be given, by way of example, one of Green's jokes— the name is mentioned on "cocksuredom" principles—to convey some idea of what may be anticipated hereafter. It was at first decided that the funny part should be left out altogether, because, as it was explained to Green, other portions of the book will read dull in consequence. As, however, Green makes it a point of honour that it be inserted, the witticism is here set down; only the reader must be pleased to remember that if he indulges in a hearty good laugh over it, and has, so to speak, a large share of merriment on account, he must not mind a paragraph or two being a little insipid here-after. But here it is, without more ado :—

Along the road marched the Tittlebato-nians on their way to Reutte. They were

4—2

pressed for time, so they walked on apace with firm and steady tread. Green's erratic legs, however, despite their owner's constant exertions, never could manage to keep the step, and although constantly taken to task by the others, the gallant gentleman was continually out of beat. Now to explain the joke about to follow, it is necessary to go into the matter somewhat circumstantially, and remind the reader that the German, or rather French, for road is *chaussée* (this must be borne well in mind, as the point of the witticism hangs upon it). The party then were marching along the *chaussée* in their accustomed light-hearted manner, singing and chatting as humour moved them. They were getting perhaps a little tired, for the walk was a heavy one, and the pace along the *chaussée* (don't forget *chaussée*, please, or the fun of the thing will be lost) was a little less regular than usual.

Said Brown to Green presently, " Why don't you keep step ?"

Said White, " I really wish to goodness you would try to march properly."

Said Black, " Why don't you chassez (be good enough to mark the word), " Why don't you chassez, and get on to the other foot ?"

Then Green, after a few minutes' pause (please to bear in mind the two words, for the whole of the witticism depends upon them) thus replied, " It seems to me that I'm always on the chassez (*chaussée*)!"

      *   *   *   *

The mountain air was so fresh, and there was so much of it too, that the halt at the top was only a short one, and a retreat down hill began without delay. Away go the hardy mountaineers helter-skelter down the incline, and bump, bump go their knapsacks, so that it is a difficult matter to pull up suddenly. The straps, singularly enough, do not hurt going down hill, so the descent goes on swiftly over the soft springy turf. Down a steep ravine, and past a clump of trees, and towards a drinking-trough, which Green and White reach after a dead heat.

"A nice place for a rest," says Green; "and here's treasure-trove." And Green waves over his head a blackened frying-pan of the latest town make.

"Halves! I book halves!" calls out White.

Green, elated at his discovery, hands the frying-pan to White, and both examine it with delight, for who would have thought of finding an article of this kind so far removed from the world and from civilization? Then White waves it over his head exultingly, to show the others what luck is in store for them.

And then, for the first time, the fortunate couple perceive behind them a low wooden hut, at the door of which are standing two sturdy shepherds contemplating the scene with a serious air. White quietly hands back the frying-pan to Green, as a disinterested clown gives back his half of the stolen goods to the pantaloon when a policeman appears on the scene, and Green, on his part, drops it as if it were a red-hot poker; and the two, having lost all interest in the matter, and having meanwhile nothing particular to do, fall to and admire the scenery with extraordinary perseverance.

However, the herdsmen proved to have been as much startled as the gallant tourists were at the little rencontre, and friendship was soon established between the parties. Large tubs of milk were brought to refresh the thirsty travellers, and the stalwart natives having been pro-

vided with cigars and brandy in return, a
happy party was soon made over a log
fire in the cabin.   Not very communica-
tive, however, were the hosts, requiring
evidently a long time to recover their
astonishment.   To Brown's remark that he
supposed the pass was not much frequented,
the answer was that, on the contrary, lots
of people came over the mountains—indeed,
some one passed nearly every day.   And as
to its being dull and lonely up there, why,
besides those two, there was a boy in the
company, just then gone to milk the cows;
so that really there could be no complaint
on the score of isolation.   It was an exceedingly jolly life, indeed, from all accounts,
because when work was done and you didn't
care about smoking or talking, you could
always go to bed, no matter what the time
of day, and it was difficult to see what more
was wanted; there was heaps of firewood

and lots of food, and so from June to Michaelmas—the period of their sojourn up there—the time passed merrily enough.

A dead halt was imminent at Obersteig, for although there were but three miles more to Miemingen, Green and his umbrella came down so heavily in jumping the last brook, that he was put altogether *hors de combat* with a bruised knee, while severe internal injury to the ribs at the same time befel the umbrella. As no conveyance or horse could be obtained to the next village, the chances of getting on that afternoon seemed very small ; as luck would have it, however, while deliberating by the wayside, there came up a waggon going to Innsbrück, and a little cart or *Rumpel-karrn* attached behind being empty, the driver was easily persuaded to allow the wounded pedestrians to be deposited therein. This was quite an unexpected stroke of fortune, and changed the aspect of affairs in a very favourable manner, for now it would be possible to reach Innsbrück · the same night, and get on to the Ziller Valley without delay. So forward started the procession, the driver in advance of the horses and waggon; then the cart with Green resting under his umbrella, like a contented Indian nabob, and in rear the line of hardy mountaineers.

There is a great difference between journeying scientifically and simply walking along *au naturel*. In the latter case you do exactly what you like; while, in the other, this is precisely what you don't do. Don't let any unsophisticated youth imagine that he can join a party of thoroughgoing pedestrians without suffering no end of hardships; for the endurance of these, he should understand, is just the gist of the whole matter; for even if difficulties

do not exist at the outset, they are speedily
created by the more strong-minded of the
party. Poor White, for example, simple-
hearted fellow that he was, fondly believed,
when he started, that he need do nothing
but follow his own sweet will on all occasions; that he would rest when tired, drink
when thirsty, throw off his burden when
oppressed, resort to his flask when faint,
and journey on just as fast, or as slow, as
pleased him. The dear fellow did not know
Brown; he was not aware that that strict
Spartan would not only presume to dictate
measures, but would see that they were
strictly obeyed. Very early in the journey
poor White was relieved of his brandy
flask, which, without more ado, was entrusted to Black, who, from his Pyrenean
experiences, was supposed to be imbued
with more strength of mind, and could be
entrusted with unmeasured cordials; while

the second bottle was carried by Brown himself. This was merely preliminary to other decrees; thus it was declared law that—

(1.) The first five miles should be performed every morning without a pause being made, whether boot-laces came undone, or straps proved obstreperous.

(2.) It was enjoined that during the march no one, on pain of being exposed to loud and general execration, was on any account to imbibe water from any mountain stream, whether under the pretence of moistening the lips, taking a nasty taste out of the mouth, feeling if the water was really cold, or trying if it was of the same kind as that met with a short time previously; excepting always when a general halt was made for repose or refreshment.

(3.) No one, on any excuse whatever, was to receive a drop of brandy from the flask except in the case of urgent necessity; and to prevent abuse, the nastiest and most unsavoury spirit, or *Schnapps*, obtainable, was always to be carried.

(4.) Finally, whenever a rest was proclaimed in the middle of the day, its duration was to be timed.

Perhaps Brown was not very far wrong when he dictated these rules; for, if framed for no other purpose than to disobey, to do this surreptitiously was exquisite enjoyment. And probably no one was happier in evading the law, now and then, when unobserved, than the great leader himself, whose long, lean figure, could sometimes be seen stooping down in the distance, to ascertain what it was that made a fountain sparkle so in the sunshine. To discover and carefully examine—in the cause of science, of course—some natural curiosity by the roadside, or to pick a botanical specimen, which required no end of circum-

spect handling, often caused the lawgiver
to pause awhile during the forbidden portion of the journey ; but who could possibly
cavil at an infraction of a rule under such
plausible and exceptional circumstances ?

From Miemingen to Innsbrück the way
is pursued *en grand seigneur*, by extra post,
with a pair of horses and postilion in brilliant uniform.   There is a train, so Brown
says, from Innsbrück to the Ziller Valley
at eight o'clock, and if this were caught a
whole day would be gained.

"How long do you allow for doing the
stage to Telfs ?" asks Brown, of the postilion.

"An hour and a quarter," is the reply.

Three silver coins, amounting in all to
upwards of fivepence, are hereupon thrust
into the postilion's hand mysteriously, with
a request not to take longer than the specified time if he loves his passengers.

Now the tipping of a postboy with a

guinea is of very common occurrence in
English story-books, and the effect produced is said to be of a very pronounced
character ; but it is doubtful whether the
response made in this instance to largess
bestowed was ever exceeded in energy. The
shuffling steeds were actually made to gallop in really quick time, although this end
was only attained by frightening the animals out of their wits, shouting, halloaing,
and horn-blowing, the postilion not being
content until the horses had regularly
settled down into a wild running-away sort
of pace. The steeds doing all they were
able, the driver then did what he could
upon the horn, and very cleverly indeed
did he handle the simple instrument. The
performance consisted in playing short passages in a loud key, which were immediately re-echoed in a softer one, an octave
higher ; the two strains of music while run-

ning one into the other appearing to come from different instruments. A charming echo-effect was produced, quite startling in its effect, and it was very puzzling at first to know how the thing was managed. An examination of the horn, however, showed that in one of the coils, for it was a kind of French horn, there was a small hole, and the explanation was, that the player kept moving his finger on and off this aperture, blowing, at the same time, loud or soft, as the case might be, and thus producing the near and distant tones.

At Telfs horses and postilions were changed.

"Shall we renew our extravagance?" asked Brown.

"Wont it be rather expensive work, if we go on like this?" said Black, timidly. "You know in the Pyrenees we never did this sort of thing."

"Well, never mind if it is," put in White, with the air of a millionaire, full of excitement and careless of the consequences.

"No, never mind, let us get on, hurrah!" cried Green. "This is the best fun we've had yet. Make him get on—tempt him with riches, bribe him with gold, so that he gets us there in time. Bestow unbounded largess, I say, and dash the consequences."

So the result was that another fivepence was bestowed in this case also, with an effect much the same as before. Four post-boys one after another were bribed in this way, and on went the party, like true Englishmen abroad, rattling through the quiet villages; past Zirl, where a stirrup-cup of capital white wine was swallowed and a further supply of stirrup-cups taken into the carriage; past the Calvary mountain, with its church and fourteen chapels; past the Martinswand of legendary fame, a

sheer precipice some thousands of feet high
overhanging the road ; and into Innsbrück
in capital style, rattling through the
unevenly paved streets and into the station
at a glorious trot, with fully half an hour to
spare—that is to say, there would have been
half an hour to spare had everything
coincided with Brown's ideas. It was true
enough so it turned out that there was a
train at eight o'clock, only it went in the
morning instead of in the evening. That's
all—nothing more than that. So there remained under the circumstances simply to
congratulate Brown, and this was done
without delay.

" What's the good of rattling up in this
insane manner, I should like to know ?" said
Green, who had quieted down all of a sudden.

"Just as I said," remarked White,
incisively ; " I knew from the first we
shouldn't get the train ; I was sure of it."

"Makes us look such fools; and all the money to the postilions thrown away," said Black.

"Yes, eighteenpence gone at one fell swoop, out of the common purse," continued Green.

Innsbrück is the capital of the Tyrol. As you admire its beautiful position, with the lofty mountain walls on either side almost overshadowing the wide streets, it is a true city of the mountains. The town lies on the banks of the Sill, at an elevation of 1884 feet above the sea, and in a situation of beauty such as few cities in Europe can boast of. It is placed   . . .*

---

* This description occupies four sides of one of White's letters to his wife, and was afterwards contributed by that gentleman for these pages. The document has since been found to be from first to last a crib from Murray.

CHAPTER IV.

TITLED PERSONAGES—A RAILWAY PICNIC—TYROLESE INNS—
ZELL IM ZILLER—ZITHER PLAYING—"AMONG THE TYROL
MOUNTAINS."

IF the French nation have a reputation for
politeness, the great Vaterland is second
to none in obsequiousness. People may
complain that the Germans are somewhat
harsh and abrupt in their language; that
they have no equivalent for the word
" sir," or " monsieur," and that they cannot
round-off brief replies or queries, or what is
still more unpleasant cannot soften the
monosyllables "no" and "yes;" for while a
Frenchman would protest "Mais, monsieur,"
or an Englishman might remark " Much
obliged, sir," the German is powerless to
employ *Herr* or *Mein Herr* in this way. But

if apparently a little uncouth in this matter,
how very much more grandiose is your
Saxon when circumstantially addressing
any great or little personage. It is not
only your counts and barons, and military
men and savants, who come in for titles
and are alluded to sonorously as *der Herr
Baron von Koeldwethout,* or *der Herr Major
von Blitzenstern,* or *der Herr Professor Doctor
Krebs,* but burghers, tradesmen, and
servitors, have also their full share of the
honours. Smith, the butcher, is termed
Herr Metzgermeister Schmidt, while a deputy
tax collector is styled *Herr Untersteuerein-
nehmer,* and as a matter of course the ladies
take up the titles, this official's wife rejoices
in the name of *Frau Untersteuereinnehmerin.*
So the guard of the train—and hence, by the
way, this digression—is *der Herr Oberschaffner*
(Mr. Upperguard), and to him it is not
unpleasant either to be called by his full

title; indeed, if you want anything at any time from the inspectors and porters, it is a good method to adopt White's plan of calling everybody *Herr Oberschaffner.* If you thus acknowledge their superiority and exalted standing, they are as a rule quite affable, and will unbend so far as to accept a cigar or glass of beer when proffered them. Only it is well to remember not to address the title indiscriminately to any official on the platform, as he may be a still bigger personage and take the salute as anything but a compliment. The same rule holds good in hotels. Here the head waiter is not unfrequently termed *der Herr Oberkellner* by native guests, and this digni- tary again, albeit a personage of tremendous distinction, and requiring due respect from all common *Kellners,* acknowledges with cheerfulness the superiority of the landlord or *Herr Patron.* Not that these grand

titles always secure immunity, for one poor
little half-fledged waiter was remarked in a
big house at Basle who could never disport
himself under the portals of the hotel near
the market-place, without being disrespect-
fully alluded to by the boys of the place as
der Herr Oberkellner von der untern-Stube
(the head waiter downstairs). Whether the
wives of the *Herrn Oberkellners* and *Herrn
Oberschaffners* take up their husbands' title
is a moot point, but one thing is very
certain, that too much stress cannot be laid
upon the fact of a man being *Ober* or *Unter*
'(upper or under), for so long as they hear
their full titles unctuously pronounced, the
good people seem to care very little what
they are called, if only it is by a good
sonorous title.

It would be scarcely fair for Englishmen to
find fault with the railway restaurants in
Germany, seeing that they are much in ad-

vance of such institutions in this country.
But we might all take a lesson from the
French in this respect, for the way of
purveying breakfasts and dinners, for instance, at Vesoul, on the line from Paris,
cannot be too highly extolled. Prosperity
to this great innovation, and long life
to its founder. How comes it that it has
not been imitated, after being in existence
so long? Surely there is no lack of patronage on the part of travellers, who thus
secure one comfortable meal, at any rate,
between Paris and Basle, with plenty of
time to eat it in. Three dishes, with des-
sert and wine, for half-a-crown, is reasonable
enough, in all conscience; and the way it
is served up is simply perfect. The guard
of the train officiates as head-waiter, and
takes orders an hour before reaching Vesoul;
he telegraphs instructions, and the meals are
found hot and ready for the traveller on his

arrival, each dinner being packed in a long
cylindrical basket, which makes a capital
table in the carriage. The wicker cylinder
opens like a rabbit-hutch, and discloses to
view tier upon tier of tempting dishes,
which are discussed by the traveller one
after the other as the train speeds on its
journey, the empty baskets being subsequently deposited at some convenient station
for return to Vesoul. The mere circumstance of having some active employment
in a railway carriage is pleasant enough ;
but when the employment consists in leisurely eating a good dinner in novel pic-nic
fashion, the time passes very delightfully
indeed. What is a dinner at Greenwich
or at Richmond compared to this? How
can the views, glorious as they are, compare to the panoramas that here move past
in·rapid succession? At Richmond, it is
true, masses of clustering foliage refresh

the eye on every side, sweeping down to a
silver river, with the tiniest of boats moving
upon its glittering surface ; while at Greenwich, again, there are the big Indiamen
moving into dock, huge screw-colliers and
paddle-steamers for ever going up and down
the stream, and loud-puffing steam-launches
darting in and out between the sailing craft.
But here, in this cosy little dining-room,
the scenery is for ever changing, and the eye
is quite as much charmed as the palate ; for,
as you lazily munch a savoury pâté, or sip
a glass of cool claret, there pass before you
in succession, ever changing peeps of some
of the prettiest country that lies around
beautiful Alsace.

Some little practice, however, is necessary in eating your dinner in this fashion.
Perhaps the best plan to pursue is that of
holding the basket firmly between the knees;
for besides keeping the table steady, it pre-

vents the occurrence of any accident which might arise from your companion mistaking your basket for his own when passing under some of the tunnels or bridges; drinking from the wrong wine-bottle by reason of the excessive vibration of the train, or abstracting the liver-wing of a fowl through absence of mind, are also possible contingencies in a merry table d'hôte of this sort. Of course it is understood that such little foraging experiments are made in quite a friendly spirit; but, at the same time, if you are hungry it is just as well to repel the kindly advances with a little firmness; and the mere expression of an irresistible inclination to insert a small fork into the forager's waistcoat is usually sufficient to persuade him to relinquish his funny intentions.

* * * * * *

From Innsbrück to Jenbach, at the en-

trance of the Ziller Thal, is but an hour's
journey by rail, and thence to Zell, at the
head of the valley, is an easy day's walk. A
quaint old monastery, enclosing a big grass-
grown quadrangle, stands at the outlet of
the valley and constitutes an important land-
mark, while the slender village steeples,
with their green spires rising here and there
above the grey cottage roofs and clumps of
trees, are pretty characteristics of the scene.
The features of the valley are soft and
pastoral, rather than grand and wild, and
afford therefore a pleasing contrast to much
of the Tyrolese scenery. The wooden
architecture of the cottages is wrought in
a most elaborate style, and the balconies,
under the over-hanging roofs, are often
masterpieces of wood-carving. Crowning
each farmhouse is a quaint belfry, sometimes fashioned in a most ornamental style,
and enhancing the general appearance of

the structure. The genuine sugarloaf hat and knee-breeches of the Tyrolese, and the broad leather belts embroidered all over most elaborately are seen here among the peasantry, the men, instead of the women, seeming to possess all the finery.

It would be difficult to find a more romantic situation than that presented by Zell im Ziller, or a more comfortable hostelry for a few days' sojourn than the Post inn. The Tyrol, it must be confessed, does not contain many first-class hotels, but what is far more to the purpose, there are capital houses of entertainment of an unpretentious nature. Thus at Zell in the Ziller valley, at Zell am See, at Fuschbad or St. Wolfgang, at Windisch Matrei, and at Niederbronn, one need not fear for comfortable quarters where the host takes a personal interest in his guests in good old-fashioned style. From the Post inn, there is a won-

derful picture of the village across the rapidly-
flowing Zill; and from the balcony, made
pleasant sometimes by strains from the guitar and zither, there are seen the snow-peaks
of the Gross Venediger group, which adjoin
the Glockner and bar the head of the Ziller
valley.

To say that you may spend time pleasantly
at the Post is to say very little; after
dinner, or rather supper, the guests' room
is considered common territory, and the
grandees of the village help the host—beg
pardon, *der Herr Postmeister*—and his
family to make up a convivial party and
spend a jolly evening. Then comes the
time for showing off one's vocal and instrumental accomplishments. The busy little
waitress, who has been running about all
day, having attended to your bodily comforts,
proceeds to do something for your amuse-

ment. And very nicely and modestly does
Julie sing the Tyrolese ballads, accompanying herself with rare skill, sometimes upon
the zither and sometimes upon the guitar, for
she is mistress of both instruments. And
then the kindly landlady—that is, *die Frau
Postmeisterin*—joins in a duet, sung with
taste and feeling enough to satisfy the
most critical drawing-room audience. Both
vocalists have indeed excellent voices, and
they sing moreover with much expression.
The jodeling is exceedingly clever, and the
way in which the voice is thrown up into
the falsetto, which is the peculiar feature
of Tyrolese singing, and brought down
again into the natural register, is quite
artistic.

The performers had not learned from
notes, neither could they read music. The
songs are mostly handed down one to

another *vivá voce*, children learning them
from infancy. In marching along the valley
in the morning, hard by a wayside cottage
were four little children sitting in a waggon
by the road, singing away with all their
might. Upon seeing strangers they suddenly stopped, and it required much en-
couragement before they would go on again.
"Singt, singt doch, wenn ihr singt, so be-
kommt ihr Kreuzer," was Brown's exhorta-
tion, and at last, by dint of a good deal of ur-
ging on the part of Green, who used his alpenstock as a bâton and imitated a jodel as far
as he could manage it, the little quartette
was prevailed upon to go on. They sang like
thrushes, with an extraordinary amount of
energy; their tiny voices, having no break,
would only give an incipient jodel, but the
performance was most spirited and satisfactory. And so they were all made happy,
and their mother into the bargain, with a

Kreuzer apiece (about a penny altogether), and sent home rejoicing.

But to return to the Post inn. One pretty air that was sung, "Die Berge von Tirol"—

DIE BERGE VON TIROL.

Schaut der Jä - ger in das Thal, sieht der
Senn' - rinn treibt die Kuh·lan aus sucht dem
Kommt der Jä - ger im voll'n Lauf drückt dem

Son - ne gold'·nen Strahl denkt er an die Sen - ne -
Jä - ger an schön Strauss, steigt glei auf die Al - ma
Diandl a Bus - serl auf sagt schön's Diandl sei so

6

rinn singt mit fro - hem Herz und Sinn denkt er
rauf sucht den Jä - gers - bua glei auf steigt glei
gut steck den Strauss mir auf'n Hut sagt schön's

an die Senne - rinn singt mit fro - hem Herz und
auf die Alma nauf sucht den Jä - gers bua glei
Diandl sei so gut, steck den Strauss mir auf'n

Sinn Diandl wie ist mir so wohl   Auf den
auf Diandl wie ist mir so wohl   Auf den
Hut Diandl wie ist mir so wohl   Auf den

Ber - gen in Ti - rol Diandl wie ist mir so
Ber - gen in Ti - rol Diandl wie ist mir so
Ber - gen in Ti - rol Diandl wie ist mir so

wohl auf den Ber - gen in Ti - rol tra la la
wohl auf den Ber - gen in Ti - rol tra la la
wohl auf den Ber - gen in Ti - rol tra la la

li i di dri a o i tri - a o i i tri
li i di dri a o i tri - a o i i tri
li i di dri a o i tri - a o i i tri

6—2

ri i ro i tra la la   li li ti   tri a ro i   ri
ri i ro i tra la la   li li ti   tri a ro i   ri
ri i ro i tra la la   li li ti   tri a ro i   ri

tri a ro i tri la i   o.
tri a ro i tri la i   o.
tri a ro i tri la i   o.

was evidently a great favourite, for the
audience listened with wrapt attention, and
encored it more than once during the evening. One song succeeded another, so that
the performance became quite a concert.

And meanwhile some capital Voslauer, both white and red, afforded a solace to thirsty souls, and accompanied the zither-playing exceedingly well. Not, be it understood, that all Tyrolese ballads are sentimental and lachrymose, like most mountain ditties; on the contrary, there are some of a very humorous turn, while others again are composed apparently for the only purpose of frightening people out of their wits. But whatever the nature of the song, the Voslauer forms a right suitable accompaniment.

After the singing and playing, hunting stories came next in importance, and these were told with much circumstance and description, for the Zillerthaler, he would have you know, is a great sportsman. The roebuck and the chamois are the principal game, and, as in England, poaching seems to be carried on with a good deal of success, keeping up a real excitement among the gamekeepers. One would hardly think that it would pay a hunter to go an arduous mountain excursion for two or three days, over crags, rocks, and glaciers, to hunt stealthily for chamois; but so it is, and the traps and snares laid for these wily creatures are said to be most successful in their purpose. Some of the snares are so constructed as to put up a signal when a chamois is taken, and the poacher has simply to look out every morning to see whether his trap has acted, while other contrivances again are so fashioned as to catch the animal alive without harming him in any way. These latter are generally laid between walls of rock well known to be the constant thoroughfare of the chamois, or through which a herd runs when discovered and driven. But it is, of course, only the skilful huntsman and practised mountaineer who have a chance of taking chamois in this way, and, as might be expected, the occupation of the poacher is a most risky and dangerous one.

CHAPTER V.

IT is a two hours' walk to the Carlssteg, a rough covered bridge (the third from Mayerhof), thrown across the foaming Zembach as it rushes through a rocky mountain gorge. The scenery has been compared to that of the Via Mala; but this will hardly convey a good idea of its character. True, there are precipitous mountain walls on either side, and a foaming white torrent, as in the famous pass of the Vorder Rhein Valley; but here the luxuriant vegetation, and the tremendous masses of detached rock through which the path leads, are the most remarkable features of the route. There is no road up the valley, but only a narrow tortuous foot-track, which winds in and out among gigantic boulders, now passing under threatening masses of overhanging rock shaped like monster grottoes, and now leading through shady recesses, the most beautiful fern gardens that can be imagined. The sheer precipices on either side constitute the upper part of the valley a magnificent defile, and the snowy peaks beyond are a fitting background to the scene. At every turn some new point calls for attention; and one is never tired of admiring the grey cliffs opposite, so steep and perpendicular in places that no foliage can attach itself. Up the valley and down the valley the view is equally fine; and the varied tints of foliage on the bold prominences impart an ever-changing charm to the picture.

It is worthy of remark that at Mayer-

hof there is good accommodation for travellers who may like to remain within easy
reach of this fine scenery; and, although
the club preferred to return to their excellent
quarters at Zell, it was not before the capa-
bilities of the local inn and dry skittle-
ground had been sufficiently tested. Skittles,
by the way, would seem as favourite a game
with the Tyrolese as it is with those fortunate gentry in London who describe themselves as rich legatees, willing to bestow
their wealth on any countryman who will
join them in a game. One sees skittle-
grounds contrived in the most impossible
and out-of-the-way places; on a country
road far from a village, or even a hamlet;
by the side of a river with nothing but
a shed or two in its immediate neighbourhood; and again on the brink of a precipice where passers-by are scarce enough,
let alone skittle-players. The skittles are

readily made by sawing up a slender fir-
tree into lengths of about twelve or fifteen
inches, and roughly pointing one end of
the log to represent the top ; while the balls
employed are generally of wood, fashioned
more or less in the shape of a sphere,
although not unfrequently large round
stones are used instead. Naturally enough
these wayside skittle-grounds are of a most
primitive description, but those attached
to the inns are often very well constructed.

It appears to be a prevalent custom in
the Tyrol to present travellers, who have
sojourned some two or three days at an
inn, with a bouquet on their departure, the
flowers being offered by the *Kellncrin,* or
waitress, just before leaving. The custom
is not only pleasant in itself, but has besides the effect of entirely removing, for
the instant, the business relations between
host and guest. It is a kindly token of

farewell towards the visitor, and seems to place him, for the time being, in the position of a private friend : a position, by the way, in which he has all along been regarded by the host and his assistants. To speak of the parting between Julie and the susceptible Green, and to tell what subsequently became of the faded flowers, would be laying bare more than it is desirable to make public; neither would it be fair to state why that youth, whose knowledge of German is very limited, should have been so emphatically pronounced, again and again, " sehr schlimm" by the fair *Kellnerin*. Suffice it to say, that an incipient scheme on that gentleman's part charitably to give his leg another day's rest was promptly frustrated by the postmaster, who provided a horse for the next day's journey with more alacrity than Green bargained for. With Brown the leave-taking at Zell was likewise a serious matter, although for reasons very different to those entertained by Green. It has been said, or rather inferred, that Brown was inclined to be careful in regard to his personal attire, and in the hope of shining with increased lustre, he had intrusted into the hands of the chambermaid his whole stock of linen to be got up with superfine care. His feelings may be imagined, therefore, when it was found that a front and four collars had been mislaid —nearly his whole wardrobe, in fact, lost in the wash. It was very little to the point to be told by Green that an English monarch— King John, to wit—had once been placed in the same awkward predicament. Brown was not to be comforted, and even Julie's flowers failed to chase away his gloomy thoughts. He was never seen to smile again until the company, like good fellows that they were, made up between them a fresh trousseau, and presented it with due ceremony to the bereaved Adonis. -

From Zell to Gerlos and thence over the Plattenkogl to Krimml makes a pleasant day's walk of about eight hours. The first three to Gerlos—a small village with a couple of simple inns—is through pine forests almost all the way, the path affording at times a lovely view of the Ziller Valley, stretching as far as the eye can reach. The steep ascent at the commencement is marked at every short interval with a picture of sacred interest, constituting it a Calvary mountain. Of these there are many to be found in this neighbourhood, and one near Mayerhof is well worthy of a visit. A chapel is situated on a solitary mound standing in the middle of a plain, and up this little hill leads a zigzag path. At every bend of the road a shrine has been built, each containing a well-executed fresco

of the various stages of the sufferings of
Christ antecedent to the crucifixion. The
chapel itself is dedicated to the sufferings
and death of the Saviour, and the paintings
are executed with a degree of art far more
befitting the subject than marks most
embodiments of the superstitious ideas of
the people hereabouts. Several really good
(speaking, as before, comparatively)paintings
covered the walls of the little sacred edifice.
Over the door was an inscription giving the
date at which the various portions of the
work were completed (the whole occupied
some three years and was finished in 1846),
and underneath the following modest
request was written :—" Those who have
contributed to the erection of this memorial
of the sufferings and death of the Lord, beg
for themselves from reverent ˙ visitors a
Pater Noster and an Ave Maria."

While on the subject of religious inscrip-

tions, by-the-bye, a curious erection may be
mentioned which was met with in one of
the villages near Lermos. It was the
figure of a saint apparently pouring water
out of a jug upon a burning house. It
was indeed an image of St. Florian, who is
supposed to guard his votaries from the
dangers of conflagrations ; and the saying
or prayer used by the people runs thus :—

> O holiest Saint Florian,
> Spare thou my house ;
> Let others burn.

The weather was a little misty on starting
in the early morning, but nevertheless it
turned out a fine day. The walk along
the side of the Heinzenberg, with the
Gerlos stream rushing rapidly along far
below, was simply delightful. A village
schoolmaster was getting his flock together.
He paced slowly along, pipe in mouth, and
in cap and shirt sleeves, while the children

scampered about around him. A little while afterwards there came along another little group.

"Where are you off to?—to school?" they were asked by Brown.

"Yes," they replied.

"The master is there, and you will be late."

Probably the pronunciation of this last sentence did not approve itself to the village intellect, so the warning was repeated with rather broader vocalization.

"The master is there."

One little girl suddenly caught the meaning.

"Is' er scho' da," she said, with an expression of juvenile terror in her face; and without more ado they ran off scampering down the steep path to the village like frightened goats. Evidently the virtue of punctuality is enforced by the dominie with the cap and pipe, in the mountain village of Heinzenberg.

From Gerlos to the Plattenkogl, the country is of a wild, inhospitable character, and the path being badly marked, a guide is necessary to point out the way. The last climb to the crest of the mountain is tough work, over ground that might, without exaggeration, be called rough and lumpy. But those who love snow mountains will not regret the trouble of ascending, for the frosted peaks and glaciers closing round one at every step are wonderful to behold. The Dreiherrnspitz, the Gross Venediger, are both visible, and far away in the valley are the three gigantic cascades of Krimml.

Green's horse was on the whole a very good charger, although, as it turned out, the owner was a far better one, for he demanded and received ten florins for taking the gallant equestrian to the top of the

Platte. However, the affair was cheap to
Green, who, as he rode proudly through the
villages with spear replaced by alpenstock,
looked a right-trusty knight, barring a little
untidiness about the bluchers and stockings.
With the guide's black frieze coat buttoned
closely around him, for it was very cold, and
his dark felt hat, he might have been taken
—at a distance, of course—for one of the
Black Brunswickers, despite what his companions, envious of his elevation, said to
the contrary. A remark about somebody
resembling "an undertaker with a smack of
the costermonger," caught Green's ear once,
though of course they may not have been
alluding to him. But, truth to tell, the
pedestrians were rather hard upon poor
Green, who, riding in front, came in for a
great share of attention. Even his frequent
attempts to warm himself, his endeavours to
chase away the cold by repeated applications

of the brandy-flask, did not escape their criticism, for it led White to remark that if matters went on like this, the cavalier must shortly exchange his horse for a shutter. This occasioned a smart interchange of love passages, and but for a sudden downpour of rain which effectually put out the brilliant flashes of wit, the language might have gone far beyond parliamentary limits.

Fortunately for the travellers there were several huts upon the Platte, and in one of them a fire was soon set a-blazing by its solitary inhabitant, who employed a wooden blowpipe some three feet long in lieu of bellows. Sitting round the embers, one's clothing soon dried, for the current of air, already quite perceptible through the rafters at ordinary times, became, in the presence of a roaring fire, a perfect ventilating shaft. Luckily there were half a dozen chimneys, so to speak, instead of only one, so that there was no decided direction for the blast to take; otherwise it would have gone hard with the stools and tables, let alone the live stock, on the mud floor of the cabin, which must inevitably have been swept up the flue. But even this atmosphere was not fresh enough for the *Senner*, or cowherd, for he kept his stock of milk in an icy cellar underground; and the shivering pedestrians were regaled to their hearts' content on cream ices. In return for his hospitality, the man had a taste of whisky proffered him, a short harangue upon its superlative qualities being first made to convince him that it was no common *Schnapps*, but something far beyond that; indeed such an idea was produced upon his mind by Brown's long prefatory remarks regarding its strength and flavour, that the poor fellow became quite nervous over the business, and entreated that as little as possible might be poured out for him lest something wrong should happen. After taking the dose, his countenance beamed with intense satisfaction, and it was then disclosed to him that the spirit he had been drinking had come all the way from Britain. He insisted upon parading his whole store of cheese and butter, and pressed White warmly to take a dozen pounds or so of them; an offer that gentleman was compelled to refuse on account of the weakness of his straps.

To walk up the Krimml valley in the same way as to the head of the Ziller Thal, beyond Mayerhof, makes a capital excursion; and in any case the traveller should go as far as the cascades, which are but half an hour's walk from the village. The second fall can be seen in its entirety, and consequently shows to the best advantage; but the spray drenches one to the skin before it is possible to get very close, while the roaring and thundering of the falling water is positively deafening, and scares one by its force and power.

The Krimml falls are probably the finest in Germany. The torrent makes three successive and gigantic leaps : to reach the first and second is a comparatively easy job ; but to the third, or highest, a good climb has to be made, and it is impossible then to approach very near, on account of the mass of blinding spray. You may, however, get right opposite to the cascade by sheltering your body under the lee of a large rock, from over the ledge of which you venture to peep now and then, encountering a driving wind that threatens to shave the hair off one's head, and takes one's breath away, the force with which the cold spray is dashed against the face being really inconceivable.

White and Green, for reasons of their

own, went off to explore the falls by themselves, in company of a shepherd's lad, not
to take care of them, but merely to show
them the way; and White's account of
their adventures when he got back was
something awful to listen to. Unfortunately he did not transfer the narrative to
paper, and thus the reader will lose a most
graphic story; although, considering its
horrible nature, calculated to make one's
teeth chatter and blood run cold, he is
perhaps more to be envied than pitied.
As far as can be remembered of the account, there was somewhere a terrific precipice of ugly black rock, at the bottom
of which could be discerned, if you were
not too giddy to look down, a seething
caldron, into which the thundering mass of
foam and water tumbled; this was surrounded, so it appeared, by a scene of terrible desolation, slimy boulders, dank and

wet, affording a sorry foothold to any one venturing near the brink of the awful gulf. It was not clear how the valiant White was enabled to look over into the yawning abyss, for no definite details could be extracted from the wily adventurer. As far as could be made out, however, Green must have laid upon his stomach in the " cautious crocodile" fashion, and wriggled to the face of the cliff, where he held firmly in his mouth the toes of White's boots, and the latter was thus enabled to project himself over the rock, and examine, with comparative ease, the scene before him.

A great deal cannot be said for the accommodation at Krimml. The inn is an antique old farmhouse, with a wonderfully wrought balcony, albeit at present in a very tumbledown condition. But if the fare is simple, the charges are not very high, and you are well taken care of. The

only thing to be borne in mind in places of
this kind is not to come home too early in
the day, for time hangs heavy indoors.
You can retire within an hour of dinner;
and truly bed is the only warm place after
sundown, and sleep the only rational amusement to be indulged in, the resources at
one's disposal being very limited. Besides,
Krimml is essentially a village without
villagers, and, except on Sundays, the po-
pulation is confined to a small and select
company, for whose sole benefit there is a
big church, a spacious inn, and of course a
dry skittle-ground. This latter affords some
amusement of an evening, but just before
sunset there comes over even the most excited
players a peculiar feeling, causing them to
lose all inclination for the game; and it is
not long before this falling-off of interest
is found to be due to excessive cold, which
persuades one to leave off out-door amuse-

ments somewhat brusquely, and to seek a more congenial temperature under the coverlet.

If the loving four had a weakness, it was certainly that of having a row over the beds. Four people naturally enough make more noise than one; but even admitting this, the matter was scarcely excusable. Brown imagined always he had a right to choice of quarters; Black, it appeared, could only sleep in the vicinity of a window; Green wouldn't have his back to the light on any consideration; and White, bold as brass in reality, would not sleep—on principle of course—nearest the door. The consequence was, that these individual idiosyncrasies frequently necessitated an entire rearrangement of the bed furniture; and the host must often have thought, when he heard his property being shifted about over head, that his temporary lodgers were

in the act of moving with their things;
while the astonishment of the chambermaid
on entering with boots or hot water, and
contemplating the eccentric changes that
had been made, was ofttimes quite funny to
behold.   It was rarely that the party were
separated, for at most inns there were
rooms spacious enough to contain beds for
all.   No sooner, however, were the sleeping
arrangements completed by the good people
of the house, and the travellers left to
themselves, than a general *déménagement*,
amid continual wrangling, took place.   One
wanted the window open, another couldn't
see with the candle so far off, the third
monopolized all the chairs for his things,
and the fourth would surreptitiously drink
up all the fresh water, and put out the
light before the others were half undressed.
In Krimml, and other places at a high elevation, another source of discord arose.   It

was excessively cold of a night ; and, consequently, peculation of bed-covering became
rife, such depredations leading to skirmishes
and reprisals in the dark. On one occasion, when a zither and guitar in the guests'
room had attracted the attention of three
of the travellers, White was found dozing
on his back, with no less than three cover-
lets stowed away in his bed ; at the foot of
the couch was his cap and feather, mounted
upon a tall alpenstock, convenient to look
upon with pride and satisfaction during his
waking moments ; while ready to hand was
the big umbrella of the party in case of
sudden attack. Such a flagrant case could
not, of course, be permitted for an instant ;
and, without more ado, a battle royal was
at once declared, in the course of which
the Tittlebat night apparel suffered con-
siderably.

It is only the upper part of the Krimml

valley that repays walking, for after eight
or nine miles the road becomes flat and
swampy.   As far as Neukirchen or Bramberg, whence one can usually get a trap to
Mittersill, the route is exceedingly beautiful,
and all along there are peeps of the Gross
Venediger and other snow-hooded peaks.
Neither is there any lack of entertainment
on the road, and it is quite surprising how
many important houses—half farms, half
inns—there are in the valley.   At Wald, at
Neukirchen, at Bramberg, and other hamlets there is good, if simple, accommodation
to be had, and if the traveller loves rambling
over old-fashioned hostelries, let him tarry
an hour at Bramberg to study the feudal
courtyard and ruins, and enjoy the magnificent group of snow peaks presented to his
gaze.   Mine host is a cheery old fellow, and
a great personage in the neighbourhood,
with which he is well acquainted.

At Mittersill, the principal village in the valley, you come once more into the every-day world; and there is an omnibus, or *Stell-wagen*, twice a day to Zell am See. More than this, there is a state prison—an unmis-takeable mark of civilization—and a garrison consisting of three men (one Viennese and two Tyrolese, they tell you), so that naturally enough Mittersill regards itself with no little pride. Once, too, the Emperor visited the little unhealthy place, and promised to do great things for the inhabitants, and a stone even now marks the spot where he was generous enough to give vent to his good intentions. Whether they were carried out or not is scarcely to the purpose, for the people are so loyal hereabouts that they are quite ready to take the will for the deed.

The "Votivbild," or "Maeterle," as it is termed by the peasantry, is a striking feature of the Tyrolese districts. Wherever a fatal accident occurs—and these are in winter not rare, unfortunately—the friends of the deceased set up a little picture on the spot, about a foot square, showing, in a graphic manner, how the casualty happened; and generally there is appended a request to the passer-by to say an "Ave Maria," or "Vater Unser," on behalf of the departed. These paintings sometimes last fifty or sixty years, and their number soon accumulate by the wayside, for obviously during this period an accident may well happen in every village. The pictures are, of course, very crude, but they all possess that strange fascination which the description of anything horrible always excites. Now it is a man being drowned in a rapid stream; now, a waggoner being crushed by his horses; now, a woman found perished in the snow, &c. The ambition of the village artist to show every detail of the accident is very apparent, and the way in which the work is performed in different parts of the country affords much scope for study. At a point where the road crosses the stream near Mittersill, there are no less than five of these monumental paintings of people drowning, all the sketches bearing a different date. The unfortunate victim is usually depicted, not merely with a serene countenance, but with one betokening perfect indifference to his perilous position, and there is painted over his head a little black cross to show that his doom is sealed. If there are any lookers-on, they are presented in holiday attire, regarding the affair quite as a matter of course, rather with satisfaction than otherwise. At Zell am See, there is a representation of a boat accident, with a number of bodies lying upon the shore, the dead being distinguishable from the quick by the circumstance that these latter have no crosses near them. Sometimes too, in a corner of the painting, is a sketch of futurity, and figures of the Virgin Mary and other holy saints receiving the departed souls. Thus, at the edge of a deep ravine at Windisch Matrei is the sketch of a boy falling headlong down a precipice into the stream below, while on the opposite side of the bank (in the picture) is shown an angel, holding the same little boy by the hand and leading him off—none the worse for his fall evidently—to heaven, impressing one very forcibly with the idea that the land of promise is always situated on the *other* side to that on which the spectator stands.

CHAPTER VI.

A PRIMITIVE CONVEYANCE—ZELL·AM·SEE—THE TYROLESE KELLNERIN—TO PERK UP—ST. WOLFGANG—GREEN'S ROMANTIC ATTACHMENT.

THE Stellwagen from Mittersill to Zell am See is quite a grand affair, although it cannot be denied it is a long time *en route;* but of this it would be unjust to complain, seeing that the number of passengers it carries is unlimited. The amiable brotherhood alone went a good way to occupy the vehicle, and the interstices were then filled in by divers peasants picked up on the road. As it happened to be Sunday, every one was in gala attire, and the picturesque and really handsome character of some of the costumes was worthy of note. The good people one and all acknowledged the aristocratic quality of their foreign companions, and put on such strict manners in consequence that they must have suffered a little thereby. Some of them, it is true, were under the impression that they had been drinking, in which assumption they proved to be quite correct, and were occasionally in some danger of falling out during a sound sleep; but on the whole they were an affectionate lot, and the gentlemen who happened to be on each side of Brown slumbered away peacefully on his shoulders, and could not have behaved with more affection if he had been their mother. Brown scarcely sympathized to the extent he might have done, for he sat bolt upright, gazing sternly through his eyeglass all the time, and regarded the mountaineers with anything but a benevolent countenance.

There is no hurrying along in these Stellwagens, and that is a great consideration.

What is the good of rushing through a
country like a whirlwind, and tearing up
the road at a breakneck pace, as if one's very
existence depended on swiftness alone?
What on earth is the use of doing so many
miles an hour, and cruelly over-driving your
cattle? Why put your life in danger by
spanking along at full gallop? There
is nothing of this in the Stellwagen;
no risk of smash or collision. You always
drive along gently and leisurely, and when
the slightest excuse for a halt arises, if
it is only for a short tête-à-tête with a
passing villager, there a pull-up at once
occurs, and matters are gone fully into. A
few houses or a hamlet necessitates the
getting down of the whole party for refreshment; and when a change of horses is made,
three quarters of an hour is quietly passed
in the pursuit of any pastime the passengers
choose. There is a simplicity and originality

about this mode of travelling that is quite unique, and if regarded only as a change you are bound to enjoy it. The driver is looked up to with great respect as a very big man in these parts. To the casual observer, however, there was nothing remarkable in his character apparently, save that once or twice during the journey he exemplified very correctly the proverb, " Call a dog a bad name," by apostrophizing one of the horses a blank Frenchman, and then proceeding to flog the animal to his entire satisfaction.

The situation of Zell am See is exceedingly pretty. As you approach, the road runs close down to the shore of the lake, and the white church and cottages of Zell are seen standing out as it were upon a promontory jutting far into the water. On each side are dark rugged hills rising from the shores, and beyond is a rare background of silver-

grey mountains with the most fantastic outlines. At eventide the charm of these magnificent crags behind is further heightened
as the violet haze of sundown envelopes
them, and then the dainty little town
appears set in a casket of unrivalled
splendour.

From Zell there is constant communica-
tion with Salzburg in the north, so that the
town forms a capital entrance or exit to the
Glockner district. Situated as it is near
Bad Gastein, the Krimml Falls, and the
Fusch valley, it makes too a suitable centre
for excursionists, and the Post inn, if
modest in its capacity, is very good quarters.
And while on the subject of inns, something
deserves to be said on behalf of the neat
buxom *Kellnerinnen*, or waitresses, one meets
everywhere. The *Kellnerin* is essentially a
Tyrolese institution; she may be found
north of Munich, and as far east as Vienna,

but there she is simply a damsel à la mode, and possesses none of the bright characteristics of her mountain sister. In the Munich and Viennese cafés she is a perfect subordinate, and has no more to do than execute the orders of her employers and flirt with the guests; but here it is quite a different matter. Everything is placed entirely in her hands and she is in supreme command; she receives you and apportions the bedrooms, she takes all orders, she sees you are properly attended to outside the Gast-Stube as inside, she makes out the bills and she receives all moneys. She is responsibility itself, and the host and even hostess sink into insignificance by her side. A neat well-fitting skirt, short enough to show her trim ankles, is her usual dress, the bodice varying in fashion and colour with the district in which she lives; her hair is plaited and gathered up in a small knot behind, quite in classic style, and round the waist is attached her badge of office—a leather courier-bag to receive the money. The smallest wayside inn, where an occasional glass of beer is called for, and where the daily takings may be calculated in kreuzers, possesses its *Kellnerin* with cash-bag complete, and she is often the only intelligent person on the premises. Pleasant, cheerful, and business-like bodies are they for the most part, and exceedingly well-informed. Bills are as yet rarities in these neighbourhoods, and the account is usually chalked upon a black tablet that is brought to the traveller for verification. The sum to be paid by a party of four, who were rather lavish on the subject of dinner and wine (these two items together often making a total of four florins), was occasionally so large as to dismay the poor *Kellnerin* altogether, and consequently the difficult task of adding up had sometimes

to be done by the visitors themselves, who
were the cause of all the trouble.   On one occasion—it was at Zell am See—there being a
scarcity of Austrian money in the coffers,
tender was made of an English sovereign,
as one might do in a big Swiss hotel, and
this coin the waitress not only recognised at
once, but valued at its true market price by
a ready reference to the last Bourse statement in a Viennese paper.

A quaint secluded little spot is Zell,
evidently living on in the same manner as
it has done for the last couple of centuries,
a perfect Rip Van Winkle of a place.   They
have simple notions, the honest folk about
here, and the outward signs prove them
of a most simple-hearted nature.   The
arrival of the Stellwagen brings everybody
into the street, and the traveller has then
a capital opportunity of looking at the

pretty costumes, which are plentiful on'
Sundays or fête days. The blue stockings,
leather breeches, embroidered belly-bands,
and sugar-loaf hats decorated with feathers
and flowers make a smart dress for the men,
and the girls with their short variegated
petticoats and neatly braided hair, are not
less attractive. And you need not so much
mind about looking at them closely, for on
their part they take a full share of the
mutual admiration arrangement, laughing
good humouredly at the foreigners' strange
appearance, and pointing out, in loud merry
voices, to one another any points worthy of
especial interest in their attire. Under
such circumstances a tourist cannot but
hold himself a true philanthropist, giving
universal pleasure to all around him.

And the quaint signs and inscriptions in
the streets—these are worthy of careful

study.   Here is a hatter's shop with the
announcement :—

> Wir lieben Gott und lassen Selben walten,
> Wir machen neue Hüt' and färben auch die alten ;

which done into English doggrel runs—

> We love the Lord, and ever let Him reign,
> We make new hats and dye old ones again.

Then upon the wooden planks of the
houses one sees written up inscriptions,
sometimes covering the whole front of the
building—sentences *in memoriam* of deceased
inmates.   To tell the truth this custom has
a somewhat depressing effect at first, for it
is not a cheerful idea to make a dwelling
house do duty for a tombstone.   Here is a
specimen :—

Leichen Brett

M A R I E   S C H M I D T,

Died on the 14th May, 1872.

PRAY FOR HER.

The swamp at the southern end of the Zell Lake is probably as good a breeding ground for adders as there is to be found anywhere, and as no necessity exists for crossing it to get into the main valley, it is very well left alone. As bad luck would have it, however, there were several foot paths leading off into it, and this was too good an opportunity to be lost by a party of pedestrians. One of the most promising was at once selected, and within a quarter of an hour the Tittlebatonians were helplessly struggling in a wilderness of tall reeds up to their very necks, and in imminent danger of being bitten by such stray vipers as failed to get out of the way of their blundering footsteps. Time and patience, however, help wonderfully in matters of this kind, and after an hour or two the gallant fellows were out again on the high road, not such a very great distance from the spot they left it. A good-looking maiden, balancing on her head a curiously shaped vessel of water, pointed out the path, and after a few recriminatory words of a " cocksuredom" character they formed line and marched in good style up the Fusch valley, one of the prettiest and least known districts of the Tyrol.

That your pedestrian is at times a bit of a humbug cannot be denied. When you pass him in a carriage, or watch him from a window or balcony, as he swings along with surprising freshness and energy, you even then get an idea somehow that his jaunty air and elastic gait are not altogether *bonâ-fide* ; but it is only on joining the craft and getting, as it were, into the secrets of freemasonry, that you begin to find out all about it. The start is generally effected in good order, and the first half dozen miles or so are got through in

tolerable style, but after that there is a
looseness, not to say untidiness, about the
walking. One man will pound away some
paces ahead, for he knows very well that if
he dosn't keep in front, he will be hopelessly
in rear in a very little time, while another
takes a path by the roadside, looking about
for fruit or flowers, and marching forward
in anything but a soldierly manner. The
third eases his knapsack from one shoulder
to the other when the straps begin to cut a
little, and the fourth puts his hat at the
back of his head and whistles or sings any
tune he knows, or thinks he does. What
is vulgarly termed "all over the shop"
very well applies to a pedestrian party after
a dozen miles or so of uphill walking, and
to tell the truth it looks for the time
being anything but enjoyment. But don't
imagine, pray, that it is the lot of the
spectator to see them in this condition; do

not think for an instant that they are to be caught out in this happy-go-lucky state. Bless you, a herd of chamois might as soon be found dozing on a hill slope as a party of pedestrians discovered sprawling in this way over the road. No sooner is the sound of wheels heard in front or behind, or a dwelling-house spied in the distance, than a hint to "perk up" is passed from mouth to mouth, and the whole appearance of the party changes. In an instant the pilgrims are at attention, marching blithely in step and in careful swing. The carriage comes up so suddenly that the gay hearted fellows are quite innocent of its approach, and are, in fact, nearly run over, the dear boys, before they have time to look up and perceive their danger. Maybe, one is chanting a song with a merry chorus, to which the others keep time, and a second, in all probability—a simple, guileless youth, this one—is studying map and guide book so deeply that he has hardly time to look up and return your greeting. Always speak in a brisk, hearty tone, and wish a pleasant good morning to people you meet, is one of the first wrinkles to be acquired by a pedestrian, for there is nothing like a fresh voice to imply freshness of spirit and absence of fatigue. So, as you pass, one and all give a spontaneous, cheery greeting, leading you to suppose that they have walked no distance at all, and as you lean back out of window to get a last peep at them, they disappear out of sight with the lightest hearts and heels in the world.

St. Wolfgang, or Fusch-bad, is probably as out-of-the-way a spa as any yet discovered. As a rule you can get to watering-places easily enough in a carriage with but little trouble and fatigue, and to most of them

9

the journey can be undertaken by a sick
man; but to get to St. Wolfgang it requires
sound lungs and a good constitution.   An
invalid who would make the journey must
necessarily be in robust health, *Il faut avoir
beaucoup de santé pour y guérir*, as M. Taine
would say; for even if he comes up the
Fusch valley in a carriage, he cannot get
a conveyance to the Bad at the top of
the hill above.   Not that it follows, in any
way, that he must walk up the odd two
or three thousand feet; not at all, for as
the authorities at the Bad will tell you,
there are abundant facilities of transport.
There are mules, for instance—the plural
is used advisedly, because there really are
two of these animals—one stationed at
Fusch-bad, and the other to be heard of up
at Ferleiten, ten miles further up the Fusch
valley.   Carriages, indeed, would be of little
use here, for there is no proper road com-

municating with the valley, and at the spa itself above there is scarcely a quarter of a mile of level ground where a vehicle could ply.

With all these difficulties, however, bathing guests do go to St. Wolfgang, and in appreciable numbers too; and all one can do therefore under the circumstances, is to wonder how they get there. The wild ravine, at the head of which the spa is built, seems, of all places in the world, the least likely to harbour town-bred fashionables; and coming suddenly upon paniers and flounces of the latest fashion in this primitive district, works an impression on the mind such as an African traveller might feel on finding the notorious watersheds by the source of the Nile strewn with empty ginger-beer bottles and sandwich papers. There are, it is said, as many as ninety visitors at a time in summer in this little swallow's nest between the cliffs, the whole place consisting of four houses and one little shop. A series of whitewashed partitions in a wooden shanty are the baths; each apartment is fitted up in a most primitive manner, with a huge washing-tub standing in the middle of the floor, which slopes down towards a gutter running up the centre of the room. The springs are cold, and have to be heated before use; and are, it is unnecessary to state, warranted to heal as many maladies as were ever set down for cure by Holloway's Pills.

Paths cut along the mountain-side afford grand promenades for the guests, for whose benefit seats are provided where there are any natural beauties or extensive views to admire. The valley of the Fusch is surpassingly beautiful throughout its whole length, and nowhere is it seen to such advantage as from these walks. Looking towards Salzburg there are still seen the craggy outlines behind Zell am See, mountains in the neighbourhood of the Watzmann and Steinerne Meer; while up the valley are the snowy outposts of the Gross Glockner and the pass of the Pfandlscharte.

Withal a pleasant spot to tarry at is Fusch-bad, and the accommodation at the little inn—for native modesty prevented an incursion into the Establishment—is good enough for anybody. On arrival White proudly led the way—somehow White always managed to be ahead at the right time—in single file straight into the baths, to the silent astonishment of the bathing guests assembled; whose surprise was indeed only natural, seeing a group of strange beings come straight up the hill and march without ceremony, one after another, into the sacred precincts of the tubbing booth.

Interesting occurrences are rare at St. Wolfgang, no doubt, and the arrival of such out-
of-the-way-looking objects was obviously a
cause for excitement. The guests, in amazement, watched the procession with bated
breath, and for a time conversation ceased
among them, and when the new arrivals entered the washhouse in follow-my-
leader style, curiosity was strained to the
utmost. What on earth they wanted in
there, those good people, the guests could
not for the life of them divine. However,
they were left to themselves, the eccentric
beings, and allowed quietly to discover
their mistake; and presently they reap-
peared at the door, and, nothing baffled,
came out in exactly the same order in which
they had entered. The building opposite
was next tried, everybody around following closely with their eyes; and here the
Englishmen were more successful, although,

at the worst, it would not have taken long to have made a house-to-house visitation.

The dinner party at the inn included half a dozen rather prim ladies and gentlemen, with whom an acquaintance was soon struck up. To one young lady in particular—in a tightly-fitting dress of maroon, with very neat collars and cuffs—Green became immensely polite, the few words of German that he knew being eked out with much skill and cunning. The dishes in his neighbourhood were at once monopolized by him and handed to the fair one, who, at first a little coy at the advances of the amiable Englishman, soon took matters with perfect equanimity. There was, of course, no great harm in paying attention to so eligible a stranger, only Green was so demonstrative in his compliments whenever he began, that he always became the centre of attraction under such circumstances.

Talking in a loud key the whole time, and floundering all over the table with his bad German and worse French, he monopolized everything and everybody, so that one was not sorry when dinner ended, and he and his charmer went off to continue their tête-à-tête under the porch. The girl was certainly very intelligent, for she understood at once all Green said with a readiness and vivacity that was quite astounding. As Green remarked at the outset, if he only had the benefit of her aid for a few days he would be able to speak German with any amount of confidence; and although the reply he received was complimentary in every way to the knowledge he already possessed, Green was far too modest to believe the damsel's flattery. This, by the way, was Green's great idea : to ingratiate himself with some of the native ladies, and in their interesting conversation to pick up

as much of the language as he could. As
he had affirmed all along, there's nothing
like a woman to help one in a difficulty;
they are so quick and ready with a suggestion, and are never at a loss to supply a
sentence when one is at fault. They seem
to have the right word always ready to put
into one's mouth, for they guess beforehand what reply will be made to their
question. It was quite different to speaking to the blockhead peasantry, who never
could understand even the most simple
matter that Green asked them, and who
usually regarded him first in stolid silence
and then with idiotic laughter; you had
no patience with them, they were so down-
right stupid.

On the other hand, Green's fair lady
possessed an intelligence and wit that was
simply surprising; and there is no knowing
how long the gallant fellow would have

kept up the conversation, or how far matters would have gone, if there had not
appeared from the doors of the Establishment a tall, bony gentleman, with a straw
hat and goatee beard, on whose arm leaned
a dashing, middle-aged lady. At the sight
of these Green's fair companion rose suddenly, with the remark, in very good
English, "I must go now," and fairly ran
away. She was an American lady's maid.

CHAPTER VII.

FERLEITEN—TYROLESE GUIDES—THE PASS OF THE PFANDL-
SCHARTE—A PICNIC ON THE SNOWFIELDS—THE PASTER-
ZEN GLACIER—CHAPEL OF ST. BRICCIUS—HEILIGENBLUT
—DINING IN STATE.

ALONG the valley to Ferleiten is a
delightful stroll of a couple of hours,
with a broad panorama of snow mountains
in front, benches being placed at intervals to
mark the more eligible points of view. On
the last wooden seat as you turn the corner of
the valley there is an inscription to the effect
that it is the first and last peep you will
get of the Fusch—a warning which every
traveller will take to heart before proceeding
further. Then the way becomes a little
more rugged and difficult, for this is the
limit of the promenade made for the guests,
and a little further on the path crosses the

stream and joins the main thoroughfare up the valley.

It will be difficult to give the reader a true idea of Ferleiten, especially when seen under the influence of bad weather, for a more depressing, God-forsaken scene it is hardly possible to conceive. Three or four barn buildings, not actually in a tumbledown condition, but, at any rate, in a dilapidated state and fast rotting away, must be imagined, standing among dirty puddles and noisome dunghills. With the exception of one, the half-dozen hovels are built with their backs to the pathway (it is very questionable whether they have any fronts), and this one, the inn, has a lop-sided and worm-eaten old balcony, whence the bleak, dreary scene may be viewed in its entirety. There is not a sound to be heard, not an inhabitant to be seen, and the desolate character of the spot gives rise to a sense of general depression. What would happen if one were detained for more than a night in this dull hole, it is impossible to say, for the Salle-à-manger is crowded with four people in it, while the loft, which is planked off into partitions to serve for sleeping apartments, possesses but one solitary virtue, that of inducing the occupant to rise by times in the morning. With all this, however, the hostess is a willing, goodnatured body, and, in fact, as far as kitchen and attendance are concerned, there is no need to grumble. Only you are very glad to be off out of the place in the morning, and willing to start away at any untimely hour that the guide may suggest. To tell the truth, Ferleiten is never seen to such advantage as when, after an hour's climb, you look back and see far below you the little buildings like toy models set up upon a strip of grass-green carpet.

In a mountainous country, the pedestrian's efforts seem to be confined to running valleys to earth, if one may use the expression. First of all it was the Ziller valley that was treated in this manner, then the Gerlos and Krimml valleys, and now a dead set is to be made upon the Fusch Thal. Let them be ever so long and ever so tortuous, they are soon made an end of with time and perseverance. The Fusch Thal ends in a sharp comb between two peaks, termed the Pfandlscharte (some 9000 feet English), and over this a way leads to Heiligenblut by the side of the famed Pasterzen glacier. If you take the Johannis Hütte, or hut, on the way at some elevation above the glacier whence its whole length and full splendour can be seen with advantage, ten hours' walking is necessary, so that the journey may be considered a very good day's walk. A second and more easy route to Heiligenblut is over the pass of the Hochthor.

The guides in the Gross Glockner district are appointed by Government and controlled by printed 'regulations. The book they carry contains the most minute details regarding their duties and obligations, and a complete description of the man's appearance is entered for the satisfaction of the traveller, so that it is a matter of certainty that the bearer of the book and licence is their proper owner. The particulars were copied out accurately into Green's note-book, who made it his duty to compare them very conscientiously with the original, for there was no knowing (as he timidly intimated) what might become of them among the lonely mountains if they trusted to any one whose character did not bear the strictest investigation. So to the poor guide's dismay, each particular was confirmed by Green as far as possible before

proceeding, the details given in the book,
being as under :—

Name . . .	A. B.
Year of birth	1840.
Religion . .	Catholic.
Height . .	middle.
Face . .	long.
Eyes . . .	grey.
Eyebrows .	brown.
Nose . . .	pointed.
Mouth . . .	proportionate.
Hair . . .	blonde.
Teeth . .	good.
Beard . . .	none.
Particular sign	none.

There is something about the goodhearted
Tyrolese—their simplicity of manner and
delight in chatting and supplying you with
information—that contrasts very favourably
with the manners of the Swiss peasantry.

Travelling has become such an institution in Helvetia that tourists are simply regarded as so much currency in trade, as much as possible being obtained out of the animate goods, as they pass from hand to hand, as if they were bales of cotton or sacks of coffee. In the Tyrol, simply perhaps because the country is more untravelled, matters are widely different. Your Tyrolese host has always a friendly interest in your doings, and there are not so many travellers but that he can have a personal chat, and give you his opinion on the politics of European powers. In any *Senner-hütte*, or shepherd's hut, that you enter, you are always welcome, and the occupants are in a general way most simple and obliging in their relations to strangers. A basin, or rather a tub of milk, you are always heartily welcome to, and often to an unlimited supply of butter and cheese besides, any modest gratuity being

10

accepted with thankfulness. And if you will but condescend to sit down for an hour, the good folks are truly pleased, and while sucking quietly at their big pipes, will listen with extreme satisfaction and attention to any news you may give them. Their modest bearing and hospitable character prove how glad they are to see you, and makes one quite regret when it comes to parting again. It is the same if you go into a cottage to inquire the way, or ask it of some villager; you are regarded somehow as honouring the household or individual in the highest degree, and it is with no little delight that they give the information asked for. Of beggars and cretins the Tyrol is singularly free, and this fact alone contributes in no little way to the enjoyment of a pedestrian tour.

A climb of about four hours brings you to the snow, and the top of the comb is reached in an hour more. There are no difficulties to be overcome, and no danger to be feared from crevasses. There is one broad uninterrupted field of snow before you, with undulations as smooth as those in any bit of country in England; it is nothing but snow, snow, as far as the eye can reach, except where rocky crags, black and grim, pierce through and rise above the level of the spotless coverlid. As you arrive at the top, and make your way further into this frigid world, the charm becomes even greater. The wide expanse of snow-fields afford a scene such as one only meets with on the higher Alps, and the sharp precipitous rocks which rise from the smooth white surface, enhancing the purity of the snow and ice, enable one to form some sort of estimate of distance. In the plains up here, you seem at times to be cut off altogether from the ordinary world, of which there

10—2

is not a vestige to be seen, for look in whatever direction you will there is nothing but one smooth sheet of white, covering everything but the rocky crags close at hand. Until you came up here you had no idea that there were so many peaks and prominences in the whole world, but now the earth appears to contain little else; and as for plains and plateaus, their existence cannot be believed in for an instant. Mountains, big and little, have grown up suddenly on all sides during the few hours of your ascent, and as if by magic the whole aspect of the earth is transformed.

And this is not the only change that is wrought, when, after an arduous climb of five hours, you come tired and hungry to the top of the Pfandlscharte. The magician's wand has done some very practical conjuring besides, for it has converted the coarse victuals carried by the guide into a repast of the most recherché description. What on starting had been but cold flabby veal, turned out at lunch to be a sort of *galantine de veau*, while the brown bread, tainted with aniseed and fennel, had become equal to the best cottage loaf ever baked in an English farmhouse. And as to the red wine, old Assmannshäuser of the finest vintage could not have compared with it, and curiously enough it was found too to be already iced, particularly cool and welcome to a fevered palate. Never was there a gayer picnic, never a banquet more enjoyable. Some granite slabs free from snow, which doubtless had served the purpose many times before, made capital seats around the dinner table, this being covered with a cloth literally as white as snow. In such a delightful situation, and under such circumstances, it was not difficult to raise one's spirits; and if only, as Green suggested, a hot-air apparatus could be devised to create a warmer atmosphere, there would be nothing left to wish for.

To get to the Johannis Hütte it is necessary to descend some thousands of feet, and mount again, for a deep, precipitous valley divides the Pfandlscharte from the Pasterzen Glacier. But the labour of making this détour is well repaid, for more charming ice fields than those which sweep down the side and front of the Gross Glockner it is impossible to imagine. From top to toe you see opposite you this peerless mountain of the Tyrol, a gigantic cone of pure ice and snow, and not alone, but in company of other giants. Above the Hütte, the Pasterzen is of a pure virgin white, but below it breaks up into huge crystalline masses of translucent emerald. Big black rocks on either side, and patches of blue sky above, contrast with the cold lustre of the glistening ice crystals, and enhance their transcendant purity; while rays of sunshine, striking aslant through a gap in the mountains, cast a band of dazzling brightness across the sea of ice. The glacier encircles the rocks at one's feet like frozen billows, and one feels tempted to descend, as it were, to the beach and toy with the glacial water. The panorama of snow landscape is unbounded, and when thus partially illumined by the sun it presents a scene of surpassing loveliness.

Near this spot, and overlooking the snowy region he loved so well to explore, is a monument to the memory of Karl Hofmann, an enthusiastic mountaineer and student of Natural History. For three consecutive seasons he devoted himself to the exploration of the Glockner group; and a volume has recently been published containing an account of his travels and that of his companion Stüdl; the work forming, indeed, the best authority on these mountains.   Although quite a youth in years, he followed out his scheme of investigation with singular zeal and ability, and set at rest many moot points regarding this group of peaks, of which little definite was known until recently.   Karl Hofmann died in 1870, fighting in the ranks at Sedan.

What a favourable site the foot of this glacier would be for a Zermatt or a Chamouix!   It is very strange that no canny speculator has taken the matter in hand already, for the locality is not such an out-of-the-way place after all.   A couple of hours' descent along a good bridle path leads one to Heiligenblut, and thence there is a road to Lienz, some twenty miles off, where the new Puster Thal railway has a station.   There are stone quarries in the neighbourhood to supply building materials; there is good pasture land for flocks, and the spot is on the thoroughfare of peasantry going over the mountains. Considered as an eligible situation for tourists, it is almost unique. An hotel here would shorten the distance to the Fusch and Gastein valleys, and render these routes within the capacity of moderate travellers; while as a spot to sojourn in for a few days, it would be in its way unrivalled. The view of the grand Pasterzen of itself is worth a journey to see, let alone the glorious peaks beyond; and the excursions that could be undertaken hence within a couple of hours or so would satisfy the most ardent lovers of ice-scenery. Then there are magnificent waterfalls to be seen hereabouts, and numberless pretty views looking towards Heiligenblut, the torrent in the valley appearing like a bright thread of silver in the distance, passing over the dark green turf, while the hill-tops around

are decked with the gayest of wild flowers
of every form and tint. And if these are
not attractions enough to secure a full
attendance of visitors, no doubt a clever
doctor would very soon be able to find out
a medical spring of some kind somewhere,
which would prove efficacious, at any rate,
for minor ailments, if only, for example,
to slake a violent thirst. And, judging from
experience, that the more difficult a spa is
to get at, the more highly it is prized, there
would be every prospect of Pasterzen Bad
becoming at once a favourite watering-place.

On the way down to Heiligenblut (Holy
Blood) there is passed the far-famed Briccius chapel, now a modern white edifice,
but five years ago an erection almost unique
of its kind. Situated in a sombre forest of
pines, the walls so old and crumbling that
the building had no definite shape, wind
and weather making way through a rude

thatching of fir-branches, and running
riot in every corner, the chapel built in
memory of Saint Briccius was certainly as
primitive a sacred edifice as any to be found
in a civilized Christian country. Upon an
upright board that did duty as an altar-
piece, was painted a series of rough sketches,
telling the story of Briccius, and how he
brought the phial of Holy Blood into that
remote corner of the world; while a bat-
tered doll of large dimensions laid aslant
the paintings represented our Saviour. One
or two pigmy figures of saints dressed in
dirty tatters, that showed signs of having
been tawdry raiment ages ago, found place on
a worm-eaten plank, or table; and the whole
aspect was at once so ancient and forlorn,
that it seemed to tell of primeval times. Far
removed from human habitations, the spot
was rarely visited except by peasants making
the tedious ascent from the village.

Heiligenblut looks very pretty in the bright sunshine. The snow-capped, majestic Gross Glockner in the background stands out vividly against the blue sky; while the river Möll dashes along past the village at a furious rate, doing its daily work of turning numberless little mills erected upon its banks, and on every tiny tributary of it capable of moving a wheel of any dimensions. The pastures are fresh and green from recent rains, and the dark firs, clothing the rocks to their summits, and the universal solitude around, give to the scene a sleepy air of repose, contrasting, by its quietude, with the restless motion of the stream, as it hurries on noisily and unceasingly.

Heiligenblut boasts neither post office nor telegraph office. Happy spot! Where seemingly you may have everything done for you by machinery without having to

pay for motive power; for one begins to
think, from the number of mill-wheels driven
by the thwirling water, that the denizens
of this peaceful valley must eat, drink,
dress, and sleep by machinery; for such a
whizzing and whirling and twisting and
turning never was seen within so limited
an area. How the butterflies were flitting
about to be sure in the bright sunlight;
quite another race of them seemed to live
on this side of the mountains. Nothing
worldly here, everything as nature made
it; and, in the absence of all authorities,
letters for home have to be entrusted to
the fat and good-natured curé of the village,
who stops in the pastoral work of feeding
his brood of chickens to receive the missives,
promising faithfully to carry them down the
valley to the nearest post station the next
time his spiritual duties lead him that way.

You may know Heiligenblut by its big

church, which is, however, seen to the best
advantage from below, with the white
Glockner peak as a background. The inn
at Heiligenblut is scarcely an establishment to be extolled ; but then it may be
argued that the host is not a proud man, as
every one must admit who has made his
acquaintance. He is only happy when in
a crowded room filled with smokers ; and
from his appearance appears to be a firm
believer in the purifying qualities of tobacco
fumes as compared with soap and water.
But one must not be too hard upon the
hostelry, for the sleeping accommodation is
clean and good, and of the food there is
little to complain.

But there is one important matter to
which, by some unaccountable oversight, no
allusion has yet been made. It is the elegant and fashionable appearance of the
Tittlebat Club when they really desired to

come out strong. It was not often they evinced a desire to eclipse their fellow-creatures, but vanity is pardonable under some circumstances. It is all very well to do the bold Briton occasionally, and to show off in hob-nail boots and rough-and-ready attire, but a time comes now and again when you get a sneaking desire to take your share in the general parade which takes place, at dinner time generally, among tourists and visitors. Be it known then that each man carried at his back, made fast by a belt around his waist, a diminutive sort of pillow-case, made of thin waterproof, which served to keep from damp and damage the tourist's best coat, a garment of trim cut and costly texture, destined at well-chosen times to provoke envy in the eyes of the male, and to soften the heart and awaken the sympathies of the fairer sex. When this coat was worn in the railway, or whilst travelling, it was scrupulously covered, by Brown's orders, with the blouse or dust-coat that served for walking in, so that its appearance should not suffer from rough usage. Besides this, there was a second pair of nether garments to be found rolled up in each knapsack, and thus a complete wardrobe was at hand.   When a halt was made for the night at a more important inn than usual, or where there was a sufficiently large audience of visitors as to make it worth while, word was quietly passed to assume "Staats-anzug" (state attire), which meant that instead of appearing in their shabby marching dress, the Tittlebats were to bloom forth in their grander suit of raiment, decked with every ornament they possessed, and accoutred to the very utmost of their power.

But the reader does not yet know all.

By cunning pre-arrangement it was determined that in each knapsack should be contained two white linen fronts, and it was
these latter that put the last finishing touch
to the already very perfect costume. The
fronts were not, it must be conceded, very
extensive, for altogether it is questionable
whether the whole party exhibited between
them at any time a full square foot of linen;
but then if waistcoats are made to button a
little high, and the wearer keeps moving
briskly about, the effect produced is not so
bad after all. Brown and Black, the two
exquisites of the party, went so far as to
bring cuffs as well—big stiffly-starched ones
too—and on this account precedence of
entrée into the guests'-room was accorded
them, for by sauntering in some five minutes
beforehand, they proved quite sufficient to
take the edge off any curiosity that those
assembled might feel, and the later arrivals

11

escaped less observed. Indeed the effect of
Brown's broad wristbands, when with a
jerk of the arm straight from the shoulder
they were pulled out and shown to their
full advantage, and aided by a sweeping
glance through his eyeglass—was simply
invincible; and many a Teuton maid and
Italian signora bowed before the leader's
omnipotent sway. And, be it borne in
mind, the conquest on Brown's part was all
the more creditable from the fact of his
resources having been seriously crippled, for
as already related, a large portion of his kit
had parted company early in the tour; and,
accordingly, the straits to which the Adonis
was put occasionally were very severe. The
remainder of his effects he was naturally
enough very loth to trust in the hands of
an hotel laundress, and consequently much
of his spare time during the midday halt
was devoted to the "getting up" of his

linen. After doing the washing in some
convenient brook, a stone placed in the
sun was constituted a flat-iron, a mangle
being ingeniously contrived by rolling the
article round a smooth bit of wood and
thumping it in the manner of local washer-
women. But of all the devices originated
by Brown, that carried out with his handkerchief was the best. Only one beautiful
soft white cambric did he possess, that remained doubled up in its pristine folds as it
had come from the laundress at home; and
to this last emblem of purity friend Brown
stuck with all the tenacity of a wounded
man to a flag of truce. It was his last hope
—the only tie that bound him to fashion
and gentility. On entering the Guest-
room of an evening in his well-known
grand and lofty style, this remnant of
magnificence was taken from the pocket
and shaken out, so to speak, in the faces

11—2

of the company, and it was only after the effect had been sufficiently and fully appreciated by all present that the ornament was clandestinely refolded, precisely as before, and returned to the owner's pocket, to be again employed in the same exulting manner on the next occasion. It was astonishing how well that handkerchief kept, considering the duty it did every night; and really, without you watched the same very narrowly—and Brown took good care you shouldn't, by waving the symbol of gentility only from afar—the effect as a whole was most finished and natural.

CHAPTER VIII.

THE church at Heiligenblut is well worth
a visit, and from the churchyard a magnificent view is seen up and down the valley,
with the river Möll speeding on its way
as fast as it can. One should not omit to
go *into* the church and examine it thoroughly, for the building is one of the most
ancient piles to be seen in the Tyrol. It has
a history of its own too about St. Briccius,
the worthy knight who lies buried within
its walls. The story goes something as
follows : —

Once upon a time in the reign of the
mighty Emperor Leo, there sojourned at

Constantinople a goodly Christian knight called Briccius. He had come from Denmark to join the Crusades, and he was bold and brave, and served the Emperor faithfully. But a time came when Briccius felt called upon to return to his own country, and with reluctance he told his august master of his intention to depart. As a reward for past services he was directed to choose among all the Emperor's possessions anything he might wish to have. Now Briccius knew that there existed among the holy relics stored up in the palace a certain phial of holy blood prized beyond measure, and this he had often desired to possess. The Emperor knew nothing of Briccius' great object, however, and in directing the knight to make selection from the treasures, was ignorant that the existence of the relic was known to him. So when that worthy soldier waited upon his master one day and

said he had made up his mind and wanted
the phial the monarch was sadly tempted
to break his word. Still Briccius was allowed
to have the relic, and he journeyed day and
night to get back to his native land, and
place the precious gift in safe keeping.
And here it is well to state—although this
takes off much of the interest in the story—
that the holy blood contained in the bottle
was not that of Christ, as one might
naturally suppose, but had been obtained
in a most extraordinary manner from a
crucifix that was speared through and
through by an unbelieving Jew, and from
which blood had spirted on the infliction of
such insult. The Jew, it is affirmed, by the
way, was converted at once by this sign, and
became ever after a good Christian.

The knight with his trust journeyed on,
his way beset with innumerable difficulties
until he neared the Gross Glockner. He

was not, however, destined to end his travels
in peace, for some of the Emperor's subjects,
maddened by the loss of the holy relic,
pursued the poor knight without ceasing,
and to prevent the prize being taken from
him, he resolved to secret it in his body.
Had he hidden the phial in his wallet or
among his garments, it would, of course,
have been easily discovered, so, martyr-like,
he cut a hole in the calf of his leg and
hid away the bottle in the cavity. But
he had not gone far before his strength
failed him, and, unable longer to bear the
pain of his wound and the severe fatigue, he
sank down and died on the roadside. It
was here that some peasants discovered him,
and finding he was beyond hope of recovery,
they buried the corpse deep under the
sod near the spot where the Briccius
chapel now stands. But before very long
there appeared above ground, much to the

astonishment of the good-natured sextons, the leg of the poor restless pilgrim, whose body knew no peace in its resting-place. Again was the body buried properly, and soon afterwards there came up through the snow that covered the turf, three ears of corn borne upon three slender stems, once more calling attention to the godly knight that lay buried beneath.

The grandees of the district were hereupon consulted, and they repaired to the spot to witness the wonderful miracle. With the aid of a waggon and a pair of oxen the body was brought down into the valley, and behold, when they came to the little hamlet, which is now called Heiligenblut, the beasts stopped and refused to move a step further. So all that remained of poor Briccius was taken into the chapel, and the holy relic was then found secreted in the leg. A church was founded to commemorate the

event, and within its precincts the Christian
knight was laid to rest, while the holy
phial and the ears of corn were preserved
in proof of the circumstances. Subsequently
a more lofty and extensive edifice was reared,
containing a most highly wrought altar-
piece, so elaborate in design and execution
that a long period of years must have been
necessary for its preparation ; around the
handsome interior, which, considering the
insignificance of the village, is really of
magnificent proportions, are paintings de-
scriptive of the journey of Briccius, and
two organs, both good instruments in their
way, are placed opposite the altar.   And
underneath, forming the crypt, is to be seen
the original little church containing the
tomb of Briccius, while in a glass case one
may see treasured up the three ears of corn,
curiously enough as bright and golden as if
they had been gathered yesterday.

One circumstance in connexion with the
grave of Briccius is worth noting, if only
to supply guardians of similar shrines with
a hint how to keep their precious charges
intact. The wooden casing over the tomb
is said to be the third already, the two
former having been chipped up and carried
away piecemeal by curiosity collectors. Now
the present guardians of the tomb happen
to be sensible men ; and being perfectly
aware that, do what they will it is impossible to prevent depredations on the part of
visitors, and being at the same time loth
that the tomb should suffer, they have
placed, in a corner convenient to hand, a
log of wood, of the same kind as that used
for making the monument; and from this
bit of timber relic hunters are invited to
cut a slice for taking home with them.
There it stands in a corner near the saint's
grave, in quite a tempting position, so that

all who feel an itching sensation coming over them to whittle at something with a pocket-knife, may embrace the opportunity on the spot.

"A sad story," said Green, when at last every ramification of the history had been explained by an old peasant who acted as showman.

"He could not have been much of a pedestrian," was White's opinion, "whatever else he might have been. If he had a long journey before him, he might have known that cutting a big hole in his leg would interfere with his walking, especially over such country as this."

"But what business he had to come all this distance out of the way for, is what I should like to know; as if Heiligenblut were on the highway between Constantinople and Copenhagen," said Brown, severely.

" He might just as well have crossed over the Pyrenees," added Black.

" If he had only chosen the way across the Hochthor, and not come round by the Pfandlscharte, he would probably have been all right," said White. "It was there he made the mistake, I think."

" Ah, and he got stopping on the way continually, I shouldn't wonder!" added Green. "It was that, and drinking at every stream he came across, that knocked him up."

So poor Briccius obtained little sympathy from the Tittlebatonians, who one and all were disgusted at his efforts as a pedestrian.

To get from Heiligenblut to Kals and Windisch Matrei, a guide is again necessary, for in some places the path is lost altogether; and besides, if you go by the very shortest way, it is quite enough walking

for one day. It is a famous tour, this journey
to Matrei, for Nature on such a grand scale
as hereabouts will impress itself on any mind.
At one point you are almost under the
shadow of the Gross Glockner, whose snowy
slopes are within half an hour's walk, for
the Berger Thörl, over which the way lies,
is in reality a shoulder of the big mountain.
You come straight upon the cluster of
frosted peaks quite unexpectedly, a gap in
the mountain all at once exhibiting them
to you, seemingly within stone's throw. It
is as if you have been searching everywhere
for them, as in a game of hide-and-seek,
looking high and low, round this mountain and down that valley, until at last
you have hemmed them in from further
escape, and find the big white giants all
huddled together in a corner. One feels
impelled to call out, "So here you are, are
you? you're found at last anyhow;" and

tempted to urge one's companions to come on quick to look at them, for fear lest they should run away again.

The route from Heiligenblut leads up the valley and to the left across the Möll, the steep pathway where it bends round the side of the mountain being termed the *Katzensteig*, or "Cat's-walk." It is a nasty bit of climbing along this cat's-walk, for in some places the slippery rock, scarcely affording foothold, slope persistently the wrong way towards a precipitous ravine, whence comes the roaring of a torrent from whom no mercy need be expected by an unfortunate traveller. The *Leiter Hütte*, a couple of hours' walk from the village, is used as a halting-place by mountaineers desirous of scaling the Gross Glockner; and here a goodly supply of milk, if nothing else, can be obtained. Thence to the top of the pass, over loose rocks and soft snow, is about two hours more; and here it is that the finest views are obtained. Let the traveller be in no hurry to descend, for it will be a long time before he has such a fine sight so near him again. The Berger Thörl is just what a pass should be—a perceptible niche in a big mountain wall cut seemingly by an engineer, if one could only imagine so gigantic an undertaking; and it is, as you pass through this portal, that the magnificent peeps of the Glockner group, and of the charming pastoral valley of Kals in front, burst upon you. Thence it goes steeply down hill into Kals, whose church spire is just visible over a black ridge of fir trees.

There are two inns at Kals, but neither of them is pleasant enough to invite one to tarry long, except in the case of those desirous of ascending the mountains of the Glockner group. Brown, on entering one

of these inns, was met on the threshold by
a dignified lady in a round hat, whom he
asked—after the usual salutation, and with
some misgivings as to whether she was the
landlady—if the valiant Tittlebats could
rest there and get something to eat. To
Brown's surprise, she forthwith claimed acquaintance, and at once put herself upon
friendly terms with the whole of the party.
To this proceeding there was, of course, no
objection, only truth necessitated the assertion—which Green, as an authority on the
subject of the fair sex, confirmed—that her
face was unfamiliar to the members of the
club.

"Whatever the dear creature means, I
can't make out," said Green, watching his
leader and the round hat in conversation.

The good lady was not to be shaken off.

"Dear, dear, how heated you all are with
your exertions; had we not better shut the

12

window lest you take cold; and no umbrella,
too." For Green had delegated his instrument to the guide.

There was another tourist present, an
Austrian, in knickerbockers and stockings,
and grey jacket turned up with the conven-
tional green facings, and a sugar-loaf hat
decorated with Tyrolese flowers; and to
him the lady referred as to whether it was
not a long way for the pedestrians to have
come from Heiligenblut. But this gentleman thought the feat to be anything but
noteworthy, and in fact expressed himself to
that effect, poohpoohing the Englishmen's
deeds in measured and pompous tones. The
reason of this presently appeared, for it
turned out that the great man was bent
upon the ascent of the Gross Glockner itself,
and anything less hazardous was therefore,
naturally enough in his present state of
mind, not worth mentioning. Indeed, he

took no further heed of the new arrivals, but turned to the window to converse with his guide and to superintend the harnessing of a small boy who was to supply the motive power for the transport of provisions; and it was not until he had seen this victim securely strapped, Mazeppa-like, to an enormous basket, and weighted to within an inch of his life, that he turned round again to see what effect such important arrangements had worked upon the Englishmen.

White was by no means disposed to take matters quietly, and when conversation was resumed affairs began to wax warm between the contending parties; the German mountaineer taking an early opportunity to leave the room to consult further with his guides, and to ascertain for a fact whether the boy was still alive. It was then explained, for the enlightenment of the lady, that although a very good half-day's march had been ac-

12—2

complished, the appearance of profuse perspiration, which bedewed the heads of all, was not the result of superhuman efforts as she might suppose, but simply to their having been ducked just then in a stream of cold water outside.

The lady was shocked. She knew a gentleman—he was a count—who had once, only once, put his valuable headpiece into cold water, and he had immediately turned mad. She did not, of course, desire to give cause for anxiety, but what she had stated was a fact. As the result was different on this occasion, the only way to accept the intelligence was to suppose that with some German heads this might be the case ; but, so Green endeavoured to tell the good lady with all the assurance of an enthusiastic physician, that if she would only try the experiment frequently herself, get well trained to the use of cold water, and take particular care to let the stream fall just nicely on the top of the spine, she would find her senses quickened amazingly.

"Who is that lady?" Brown asked of the host, when she had gone.

"The Countess of ——," was the reply.

Good heavens! poor Green was dumb-foundered; and White only wished that he talked German so as to have bounced when he got home of having conversed with a countess. Green was not let off easily for having talked in that free-and-easy manner to so aristocratic a personage.

"You might have guessed," said Brown, "she was somebody particular; why, I could see it from the first."

Green did not recover his equanimity for some time; he could never forgive himself for tendering advice to a *gnädige Frau,* and shocking her sensitive nature with sugges-tions about raw cold water to be poured

over the nape of her noble neck. Well
might he remain silent under the circumstances.

There is a game in great vogue at Kals
which must be referred to, for it helps very
materially to pass the dull long evenings in
winter time. It is a very simple amusement, and requires but little paraphernalia.
A couple of iron rings an inch in diameter
are attached to the end of a long string
suspended from the ceiling, and the game
consists in standing on one side of the room
and swinging this pendulum as it were, so
that one or both rings catch upon a hook
fixed in the wall opposite. A good deal of
skill is required to do the trick successfully,
and many are the mugs of beer won and
lost over the game among the peasants. "Nobody," said the host, " could throw the ring
like the worthy pastor of Kals, who, whether

he used the right hand or the left, invariably placed the rings upon the hook."

In two hours you may reach the narrow mountain comb that separates Kals from Matrei—the Matrei Kalser Thörl, as it is called—the top of which is marked by a wooden cross; and probably at no other point hereabouts could you find such an extensive panorama. There are, be it known, two distinct groups, or clusters of peaks and glaciers, the one being termed the Gross Glockner group, and the other the Gross Venediger group. The Kalser Thörl upon which you stand divides these two clusters, and, consequently, whether you look in front or behind, the sight that meets the eye is equally grand and imposing. A few cloud-patches about heighten the effect amazingly, for there the snowy pyramids reach up right into the heavens, giving

rise to all sorts of fancy forms and shapes;
it is difficult, of course, to distinguish the
peaks from one another without a reliable
map, but this is a matter of lesser consequence. The green meadows and black
pine forests in the plains at their base
enhance the beauty of the snowy spires
beyond, and the tiny farms and houses
grouped about in the valleys, so near, apparently, as to be within pistol shot, induce the
belief that you must have discovered fairyland, and that these miniature habitations
and microscopic buildings are the veritable
dwellings of the elves and fays so much
talked about. Would you have a peep at
Lilliput, here it is just below you, everything
uniformly small and pretty. No big rivers
or broad torrents are there, but only
slender threads of silver, and the little village
church, perfect as to modelling, could be
shut up in a pill-box. The atmosphere is

so bright and clear that distance goes for nothing.

Green's accomplishments in the musical line came in very useful sometimes, and on one occasion it was a means of identifying a guide, by proving him, in Irish fashion, not to be the man he was supposed to be. In coming from Ferleiten, the young fellow who acted as guide, and who had been so minutely scrutinized by Green before start-ing, gave cry on several occasions to a jodel or Swiss chant, which, being rather melodious, the musician of the party at a convenient moment noted in his book. This same man having proved efficient, was further engaged to go on to Matrei, and when in the grey of the morning he came and led off the party, nothing occurred to arrest attention ; once or twice the question arose whether it really was the same guide, to which query some one made answer, " Oh yes! he is the man, but he hasn't his snow clothing on, and, besides, he has taken off his green spectacles." But towards the end of the day's work the guide began to jodel.

"Hallo," said Green to Brown, "that isn't his jodel."

"That isn't your jodel," repeated Brown to the man, as if he had appropriated something not his own.

"This is his jodel, you know," and Green turned to his pocket-book and hummed from his notes—

The guide hereupon pulled up. "That isn't

the same jodel you sang yesterday," repeated Brown ; "just do it over again, will you ?"

And then the guide repeated his jodel, Green noting it down the while, and lo, on close examination, it turned out to be another man, as well as another jodel.

" Why, you are not the man that came over the Pfandlscharte with us," remarked Brown.

"Certainly not," said the guide, astonished ; " that man obtained an engagement to go back home, and therefore sent me."

This was a little amusing, after Green being so careful too, especially as during the course of the journey all had been very liberal to him with wine and food as a reward for his civility on the day of passing the Pfandlscharte, the good man taking everything under the idea, no doubt, that Englishmen were universally generous and considerate.

CHAPTER IX.

MINE host at Rauterer's hotel in Windisch Matrei is a right merry fellow, and his inn is one of the best in the Tyrol. Coming immediately· after the houses of entertainment at Ferleiten, Heiligenblut, and Kals, one is perhaps scarcely so particular as usual; but, in any case, the principal inn at Matrei is a most comfortable hostelry. It is just what an inn should be; well furnished and cleanly ordered, with a good kitchen and active attendance; it is everything the most fastidious would desire, for there is a homeliness and cheerfulness about the place unknown in first-

class hotels. Every stranger becomes a
personal guest, and the host sits down at
the same table, to see he is properly attended to. And the reason for all this
courtesy is simply because the good maître
d'hôtel does not profess to be any other
than he really is. He is delighted with
his visitors, not only because he makes
profit out of them, but because they have
done him the honour to enliven him with
their company. Every little matter that
can interest the traveller is discussed and
brought to your notice. As you stand
under the simple portico and look up the
picturesque little street, overshadowed by a
big black mountain that threatens its de-
struction, the kindly host explains what
there is to be seen in the neighbourhood,
and apologizes for anything he deems
obtrusive, even if it be nature's fault, and
not his own. That patch of white, for

instance, which you see in a cleft of the
peak just referred to, he tells you ought
not to be there at all; it is not a glacier or
even permanent snow, and he really cannot
account for its presence, because, by rights,
it should disappear in early summer. From
some unaccountable reason, however, it has
remained this year; but, so his deprecating
manner seems to say, it shall not happen
again, or he will know the reason why.
The road is out of repair just now in front
of the inn, and this is really too bad,
because the workmen ought to have finished
the job long ago—last week at the latest;
but he will go and talk with them, and get
an explanation of the delay. If he had his
way, such disturbances would never occur;
and then finding his visitors still dilly-
dallying about the premises, he thinks it
high time they were off sight-seeing. Now,
where are you going to? What is to be

the first excursion? It will never do to be
dawdling about the inn all day; that, evidently, he would never permit for an instant, for everybody has their work to do,
and tourists must not be idle. What
do you propose to do? You can either go
to Gruben, and so to the base of the Gross
Venediger, or there is the Pregarten valley
to explore. About an hour's walk hence,
just by a crucifix, there is a delightful
glimpse of glaciers and snowy peaks. Only
you must decide quickly, or he will order
matters for you, and then there will be no
choice.

But with all his good qualities, there is
one weakness mine host possesses; it is
that of sending people up the Gross Venediger. That is, to him, the be all and end
all of one's existence. A man who has lived
through life and not been to the Venediger
Spitz may be a good man in his way, but

he is by no means perfect.   The ascent of
his big neighbour is the only thing worth
living for, and when accomplished you can
die with dignity.   It is all very well to say
that you have not the courage, nor the
means wherewith to attempt such an ex-
ploit; all this avails nothing; if the weather
is favourable you are bound to go.   It is
your bounden duty, and why on earth did
you come to Matrei if you did not mean
business ?   You may plead ignorance, and
say you were not aware of the responsibility until you arrived, but these are mere
excuses.

But has the host been up the Gross Venediger? you ask.   Well, you may put the
question, but to what end?   Of course he
has been; twice, indeed; once about ten
years since, and once only last year.   That
is to say, he has been up, but not quite to
the top, you know, but very nearly, very

nearly indeed. So close to the summit was he, that had it not been for the unfavourable state of the weather the renowned Spitz would have been very heavily sat upon for once in its existence by the daring host; but fortune favoured the big mountain, and it was let off for the nonce. But only for a very short time; and even now one may consider going twice half-way up a mountain is just as good, any day, as reaching the top only once.

But in what direction is the first excursion to be made, that is the question? "To Gruben and to the base of the big mountain, to see what it looks.like," suggests Brown; and without more ado the host takes the party into custody, and guides them up the valley to be sure that the walk is no make-believe on their part. There is no escape now, and although the Tittlebatonians had decided upon a quiet

13

off day, no alternative remains but to go
quietly whither they are led.

Up the valley under the picturesque old
castle on the hill, past some old farmhouses
and fields full of haymakers, the good man
leads the way, for about a mile, to the entrance of a deep ravine, out of which tum-
bles a big cascade.

"Now then," says the host, stopping short
and puffing audibly, "take the left of the
ravine, when past the waterfall, and that
will lead to Gruben and to the head of the
valley.   And in returning, you can choose
the other side of the defile, and thus make
a variation of the tour.   You understand
now?" turning to Brown.

That gentleman is quite confident of the
matter, and tenders his thanks; he thinks
now the way will easily be found.

"But remember," adds the careful host,
"remember to keep to the left in the first

instance, because the waterfall is seen so much better.

Brown promises that this shall be done.

"It is impossible to miss the path if you go behind that barn and cross the stream at once, but be very particular to ascend by those houses;" and then the good fellow departs, looking back now and again to see that all is right.

The day is very warm and the sun quite oppressive, the heat bearing down weightily upon one's head. To go any distance on such a day is impossible.

"Look here," says Green, suddenly becoming mutinous, "I thought we were to have a day's rest; it's too bad to make a fellow go on walking day after day in this manner. I was sure how it would be; Brown is always talking of having an easy day, but somehow we never get it.

Poor Black even broke silence and muttered something about their having taken it more quietly in the Pyrenees.

"But it isn't my fault," returns Brown, waxing wrath; "why didn't you tell the old fellow at once that you wanted to stop at home? Why, White here wanted to go up the Gross Venediger this morning when he heard of it."

White puffs himself up with much dignity after such a handsome allusion, feeling bound to support the last speaker. He intimates, with an important shake of the head, that he certainly should like to make the ascent, and that if they stop another day at Matrei, it is more than likely that he shall do so. If there is anything for which he has had an ambition in life, it is that of scaling the Gross Venediger some day.

This is more than Green can stand. "Why, you didn't even know till yesterday

that there was a mountain of that name."
White was astounded at such an assertion.
"And what is more," continued Green,
"you would not have thought about it had
not the host told you it could be done comfortably and without risk."

The Tittlebatonians were out of temper,
and their style of walking in the hot sun
was not such as would impress one with the
idea that they contemplated performing any
very daring feat just then.

Presently the barn alluded to by the host
was reached. There was nothing peculiar
about the building, but somehow it occurred
to all to step in and look at it. Whether it
was for the purpose of seeing what was contained therein, or to observe the mode of
preserving hay in that part of the country,
is a moot point; but certain it is that the
dispute came to an abrupt end, and everybody gazed around with the utmost interest.

A question arose as to whether the hay was this year's crop or last year's, and to settle this point, the party, with one accord, began to explore the cool shady refuge. No satisfactory decision could be at once arrived at, and after pinching and smelling for some time, it was determined to find out by sitting upon it. It would never do to give up so important a matter without some considera-tion, and consequently all laid quietly down to think the matter over carefully. A few arguments were advanced pro and con, but after a time each man resolved to think the matter out quietly by himself, and so all kept their thoughts entirely to them-selves. In this way an hour and more passed without any decision being given, and barring one decided opinion expressed by the scientific Green, that the desic-cated fibre was the abode of several lively specimens of entomology, no positive affir-

mation was advanced. There is no knowing indeed how long the philosophers would
have continued their profound studies,
reposing upon their easy couches, had not the
threshold been suddenly darkened by the
portly figure of mine host, whose misgivings
that all was not going on rightly had
caused him to return and search for traces
of the gallant pedestrians. Of course, profuse apologies and explanations were at
once tendered, for otherwise the good man
might have supposed that his guests had
left his implicit instructions unheeded, and
gone into the barn, as soon as his back was
turned, simply to lie upon the hay and kill
time in a lazy purposeless manner. He
scarcely listened to the explanations offered,
but stood severely at the door until all had
departed, the spiritless Tittlebats making
their exit one after another in more or less
lively fashion. And this time it was im-

possible to practise any deception, for it was
not until his guests were laboriously toiling
up the hill before him that the host again
left them to their own devices.

Windisch Matrei is not only a pleasant
place in itself, but it is moreover a most
eligible headquarters for excursions, whether
the tourist be a modest walker or hardy
mountaineer. You are in the very midst of
lovely scenes and fragrant pine forests, and
these can be enjoyed with little fatigue.
Thus, as far as Gruben—not two hours'
walk—the way is highly picturesque, the
path being a ledge cut by the side of a
frowning ravine, so steep and tortuous that
you never know how far you will be able to
proceed. The sombre walls of rock close
together so suddenly as almost to choke the
passage, and the little shelf of a path seems
at times to be lost altogether. Then the
magnificent waterfall seen from the preci-

pice above is alone worth a journey, the. fantastic shapes taken by the foaming water as it dashes against jagged rocks in its headlong flight, forming gauzy rainbows in the sunshine, looking like a glimpse of fairyland. Past Gruben you come to the very base of the mountains or Tauern, the crossing of which to Mittersill or Krimml completes the tour of the Gross Glockner very perfectly.

But this step would prevent one seeing the Pregarten valley and the fine bit of country lying between Matrei and the Dolomites in the Puster valley, and therefore one must needs be content to drop this link in the chain round the Gross Glockner, and return again to Matrei, the obligatory duty being in truth a very pleasant one:

And so the Britons journeyed back to dinner, the host being in excellent humour

on a report of the proceedings being sub-
mitted, as, by-the-bye, he need have been,
seeing he had everything his own way.
And while on the subject of meals, a word
of praise deserves to be said in favour of
the Tyrolese trout. "Will you have them
blue or brown?" the waitress usually asks
you, and she means exactly what she says.
When boiled the delicate fish are of a pale
blue tint, while fried or baked they naturally
enough assume a brownish hue. Cooked
either way, they are a most toothsome dish,
and form a welcome change to the veal and
salad which is the staple of most dinners.
There is another dish, too, that they understand perfectly in these parts—namely, pancakes, and these can be obtained when meat
and butter are not forthcoming. An *ein-
gefülltes Mehlspeise* (Green called them male
spiders), a pancake stuffed with preserves,
will satisfy anybody, and is a capital foun-

dation for walking upon. For drinking there is good beer to be had throughout the Tyrol, as well as palatable red and white wine, it being a matter for regret that the keeping qualities of the latter are not equal to their other virtues.

Dinner finished, the host had a further chat on the subject of mountaineering.

"We are going to explore the Pregarten valley next," explained Brown.

The host was by no means elated at the news.

"It will be a fine day to-morrow, I feel sure," he said; "if you want to make a good excursion, now's your time."

White had become quiet all of a sudden, for everybody knew what was coming.

"Just the sort of weather for making an ascent of the Venediger Spitz," the host continued, in an off-hand, disinterested manner. "I don't think I ever knew a day more favourable for the purpose—a clear evening and no wind."

Really one began to suppose that the old fellow received a capitation grant from government on every traveller he sent up the big mountain; or was it that like professional crammers who coach young gentlemen for examinations, he meant to advertise that out of so many visitors who had stopped at his hotel, such a number had gone up the Gross Venediger?

"I have a great mind to go," hazarded White, after a dead pause, and breaking into a perspiration.

"I will take care of your things when you are away," volunteered Brown.

"And of any letters you would like to write," said Green.

White hitched his nether garments nervously, and, looking round a little uncomfortably, gave a short cough and went

through the motions of swallowing two or
three times.

The host was unwilling, of course, to influence by an opinion one way or the other,
but it might be useful, he thought, to mention that in case an ascent was projected,
there were guides always ready and waiting.

"I only wish I had bigger nails in my
boots, that's all; I wouldn't hesitate a
moment," said White.

But this was a difficulty that the village
shoemaker would get over in an hour, the
host bore witness.

"Ah, but then again, I don't know
German sufficiently well to understand the
guides," pleaded White.

But this objection too was overruled by
the statement that the guides were an intelligent set of men, and had repeatedly had
Englishmen in their charge.

White next objected to his ice-pole, and

then to his having no snow-veil, but the
difficulties brought forward one by one were
met as soon as started ; so there was really
no alternative under the circumstances but
for poor White defiantly and flatly to refuse
to go on principle. This seemed both unfair
and ungallant : unfair because for the last
half hour he had usurped the reputation
of a bold headstrong mountaineer on the
eve of a perilous journey, and ungallant
because the fair Kellnerin, who admired him
from the first, had been delighted that this
one of all his fellows should be the
bravest and most intrepid.   It was too bad,
just as every hindrance had been explained
away, to have the champion of the company
refusing to depart without rhyme or
reason. No explanation would White
deign to offer, but he allowed it to be
inferred, by his mysterious manner, that
if people had not set upon him in a body,

matters would have turned out far differently, and that while he was still personally anxious to make the ascent, he did not do so simply and solely out of spite to the others. It was merely a matter of personal feeling and nothing else, he gave all to understand, and he stalked off to bed with lofty strides that would have made the big mountain' tremble at his approach had it been human.

As beautiful in its way as Gruben, if not altogether so grand, is the pretty valley of Pregarten. The way leads from the village over the rushing torrent, and ascends gradually through a forest of sweet-smelling pines. So densely wooded is the mountain side that in places the branches meet together and overshadow the lazy wanderer. Opposite are other green-clad slopes, whose soft outlines against the sky complete the most perfect picture of forest scenery one can well imagine. There are many attractive points along the valley, but the most pleasing of all is when you reach the crest of a hill about an hour's walk from Matrei, where the path dips down into the little village of Virgin. The spot, marked by a crucifix, is startling in its beauty. It is as you come round a bend in the road that this glorious peep is secured, and one must needs rest awhile on the grassy bank to enjoy it. On either hand are grand old pine forests, the dark mass of foliage on the steep slopes reaching to the vale below, where the tiny cottages of Virgin are grouped about in picturesque confusion. And in the background, above the black firs and waving green boughs, peeps forth a virgin snow peak confessed in all its purity and loveliness. Such a scene on a summer's evening when the gleams of sunshine are giving place to a rich purple haze that literally fills the valley with colour, is one no mortal can behold unmoved.

And as one gazes upon the beauteous picture, there comes down the path, with painful and halting step, an old woman bent double with age and infirmity, with a face that long ago lost its comeliness and now embodies only what is ugly and loathsome. Glancing neither to the right nor to the left, the poor creature shuffles on her weary way, and as she reaches the favoured spot she too makes a pause of a few moments. Can it be, think you, that she appreciates the beautiful landscape? can she too take delight in the divine panorama before her? No, her stay has a very different meaning, for it is only when she reaches the crucifix itself that she comes to a halt. Glancing up at the holy emblem, she mutters a short prayer, and then fondly taking the rough timber in her hands she kisses it reverently

14

and passes on, going away slowly down hill to her home. A more simple and touching act of devotion can scarcely be conceived, nor could a more fitting spot have been chosen for its enactment.

And now the sun has gone down night comes on very fast, for twilight is of but short duration in these deep valleys. As you stroll home in the dusk the woods resound with quaint sounds and utterances, and fireflies flash across your path like eccentric will-o'-the-wisps. It is dark before Matrei is reached, and the pleasant hotel sighted once again.

If White ever encountered a difficulty in his life it was that of writing a letter. His talents for story telling were of a far higher order than his caligraphic attainments; and therefore the letters sent home to Mrs. White could scarcely have been so interesting to read as the exciting adventures her

husband was wont tell of. When the Tittlebatonians sat down of an evening to
relieve their over-charged brains of the
interesting experiences treasured up therein
and transfer them to paper, the first to
desist and come to a full stop was the
bravest of the party. While others would
scribble away sheet after sheet, reading over
with quiet satisfaction what they had written, as if it was the finest and most humorous composition in the world, never
taking their eyes off their paper, but chuck-
ling inwardly at every word as they wrote
it, White would look up, after laboriously
filling in date and address, and making
some stereotyped commencement, quite unable to get any further. He would glance
first at one and then at another; and
after thinking restlessly over the matter
for some time, would at last come out

with: "I say, you fellows, what shall I tell my wife?"

The interruption was exceedingly provoking at times, but it soon was regarded as a matter of course, and the suggestion invariably given was to describe one of the numerous adventures in which he, White, had, according to his own showing, played the part of hero. But somehow that gallant gentleman never could be brought to put upon paper, much more send to Mrs. White, any account of his daring and intrepidity, either because of his innate modesty, or on account perhaps of his being unwilling to make his partner anxious about his safety. As an amateur farmer, very knowing on the subject of crops, the matter ended by his epistles containing descriptions of large-sized turnips and tremendous wurzels which he had seen, varied occasionally by facts in natural history regarding horrible snakes and terrible vultures he had met with ; and not unfrequently finishing off with some local legend he had heard of, detailed with such precision and circumstance, that it read like an event that had happened yesterday.

CHAPTER X.

THE road from Windisch Matrei to Lienz, in the Puster valley, is a pleasant one, the distance a march of five hours. Looking back when you have left the village a little way behind, before you enter the wood, the snow-peaks at the head of the Pregarten valley are seen to stand out bold and clear, with the old-fashioned houses of Matrei forming a happy foreground to the picture. The hamlets and villages you pass all possess the same quaint antiquity, and the inhabitants suit them in every way. They heed little the strangers that pass by, and take no interest in the reasons of their coming and going. To them it is of little moment how the traveller speeds on his way; and only at one point along the route is there any chance of obtaining transport. So unused, apparently, are they to the ways of strangers, that at a little inn on the roadside the host, who happened to be outside his house, could not conceal his excessive delight at the prospect of entertaining such aristocrats as the Tittlebat Club, and some time elapsed before he could realize the fact that they really meant to bestow their patronage upon him. That four travellers, and foreigners too, should come to him, of all men in the world, and desire entertainment, was to be regarded as something more than luck; and the way in which the old gentleman bustled about and kept the household in a state of excitement, was an experience tó remember. Not that he did anything himself in the way of ordering matters, his wife and the *Kellnerin* did that; but the delight and the responsibility he felt was too much to let him remain still for a single moment.

Now what would they desire to eat? what would they have to drink? were they tired? had they walked far? what country did they come from? what made them choose that particular inn? where were they going to? and many other questions were asked. His chief anxiety was to find out the nationality of his guests; and it was only on demanding the bill that the brave fellow became grave and silent. The account required much elaboration and thinking over, and it was only after a long consultation with various members of the household that the document was presented with a show of much pride and importance. It was a curiosity in its way, worked out by the united efforts of host, waitress, visitors, and *amici curiæ* from the village, upon a bit of brown paper some eighteen inches long and nine broad, with the aid of several ounces of chalk.

Painful as may be the circumstance, duty compels the mention in this place of an event which it would have been well to suppress and omit altogether from these chronicles. However, it shall be briefly told. As already stated, Black, as a reliable custodian, had been entrusted by Brown with the second brandy flask of the party; and this office of guardian he fulfilled so religiously, that, despite the entreaties and threats held out occasionally both by White and Green at trying points of the journey, not a drop of the liquor was forthcoming from the tightly screwed-up apparatus. The most ingenious tricks and schemes were devised to get a pull at that sacred bottle, but all to no purpose. Green had been known to get up surreptitiously in the dead of the night to obtain possession of the coveted trust; and White on more than one occasion had essayed by brute force to get a taste of the liquor; so that at last it became a question to Black whether he would not have to imitate the example of Briccius, and carry the flask in his leg, to preserve its contents intact. But fate was against the Pyrenean explorer. It was just before reaching Lienz that the two good-for-nothings, caring little for honour or prestige, determined to make one final and concerted onslaught upon poor Black, and either succeed or die in the attempt. Brown was allowed to get on well in front, and gradually Black dropped behind with White, who narrated, for the purpose of entertaining him, one of his most exciting adventures. At a prearranged signal, Green, who had been marching in front with the leader, also halted for the purpose ostensibly of lacing his boots, and as Brown disappeared out of sight at a bend in the road, the little bottleholder was fallen upon by the two ruffians.

"Now, come, let us have a drop out of that at once," cried the conspirators, turning upon their unoffending companion.

Poor Black saw in a moment it was all over with him. However, he attempted a parley. "If you are thirsty, try munching a bit of stale bread. It is a capital thing for bringing back the saliva to a dry mouth. I know when we were in the Pyrenees——"

"Oh, bless the Pyrenees!" said White, impatiently, only he used a naughtier word than "bless;" and, without much ceremony, Black was despoiled of the coveted flask, which was forthwith emptied by alternative sups by the two outlaws. Black sat on the bank and contemplated the sacrilege in speechless surprise, mechanically receiving back the empty bottle as if the whole thing was a dream. And when they caught up to the great leader afterwards, the poor fellow never once alluded to the matter, although the exuberant spirits of the other two, and the buoyant manner in which they marched along ahead even of Brown himself, puzzled that gentleman exceedingly, and caused him more than once to wonder what on earth had happened.

Five years ago Lienz was an obscure little town, through which a diminutive *Eilwagen* travelled once a day, connecting the railway stations of Villach and Brixen on the Brenner; but time has worked wonders, and it is now an important point upon a railway, set down in the time-tables in big letters, and furthermore honoured by the train stopping some minutes at its newly-built station. The whole town, it would appear, has been in a torpid state since the time of the Crusades, and bears throughout signs of Eastern architecture. Even now the inhabitants are scarcely wideawake enough to appreciate the dignity of being connected by railway with the Brenner line. It is true the good people assemble in force at the station whenever the trains arrive or depart, which is, by the way, only twice a day, but there is no evidence to warrant the belief that any of them so far have purchased a ticket. They are willing, of course, to countenance and support the thing as far as their presence goes, but naturally enough a dislike exists among them to be the first to risk their lives in the new-fangled machines. So they have built a large restaurant near the spot, together with an extensive skittle-ground, and here they can have all the excitement of the affair without running any risk, being always close at hand, not to lose the chance of seeing even a luggage train pass. When the engine is heard from afar, skittles and beer are at once forsaken, and faces are flattened against the palings, while, with serious and intense interest, all watch the wonderful line of carriages approach along the rails, and examine the passengers—if there are any—with unmistakeable awe and admiration.

Those whose only experience of trains and railway traffic is confined to half a dozen lines in England, possess no idea whatever of the fearful responsibility and excessive anxiety which some of the minor branches on the Continent involve. Let no one imagine for an instant that he knows anything about railway travelling simply because he has journeyed by some of the quick trains in England. There never was a greater mistake. Take, for instance, the

morning-express to Scotland on the Great
Northern; why, here there is absolutely nothing at all to see calculated to impress the
mind with the importance of railways and
railway officials. There are simply a dozen
carriages and a locomotive up at the further
end of the big station, and as passengers
arrive, they are let into compartments
marked "Aberdeen," "Edinbro'," "Glasgow,"
&c.; a few inspectors moving noiselessly to
and fro the while. Presently, the hour of
ten is indicated by the clock on the platform, a guard whistles, and in another moment the train quietly glides away, getting
up a swinging speed of some fifty miles an
hour as soon at it is clear of the bricks and
mortar. Say what you will, the whole thing
is exceedingly tame—flatter than walking.
Now, hereabouts it is quite a different
matter; nothing is done without proper deliberation and dignity, and even the trains

themselves are never seen in an unseemly hurry, but progress—*immer langsam voran*—with measured step and slow. But it is the officials, after all, that impress the stranger most vividly; the jaunty cut of their smart blue uniforms, their bright buttons and slashes of silver lace, cannot but fail to attract the eye, for officers in a crack cavalry regiment would be envious of such brilliant and elegant costumes. Then their frank and gentlemanly bearing is quite in keeping with the splendid exterior.

It will never do, however, to enter a carriage without first craving permission, and in the case of humble passengers many complicated details as to early life, parentage, or of some such nature, have to be gone into before the boon is granted. And when you come to think of it, it is really very kind of these good-natured gentlemen to take any interest in the matter at all, for it must be a great annoyance to them to be constantly obliged to answer questions and look after low-class passengers at every little station. It is rarely that they are put out of temper; yet only fancy a dirty peasant tapping you on the sleeve of your azure uniform just as you are lighting a cigar, or sipping a glass of beer with a friend, and asking you to put him into the proper carriage for the Brenner. That the man will be sent off about his business with a good round oath is what you might naturally expect; but no! the official is not at all offended, he good-naturedly points to the train across the rails and intimates that he the passenger may open the door for himself. Then, besides the annoyances from travellers, there is the whole responsibility of starting the trains upon their hands, and this is no insignificant duty, be it known. No less than four distinct and separate operations

15

have to be gone through before a clear start can be made, exclusive, of course, of imbibing beer and *Schnapps*, or taking other refreshment. The first thing, and perhaps the most difficult, is to collect passengers who have strayed into the refreshment-rooms, and this takes time; consequently its accomplishment is effected some time before the official period set down for starting. The troublesome travellers are checked in their disgusting attempts to swallow food and drink in a hurry by a loud and spasmodic ringing of a bell, and after being chased into their compartments and summarily locked in, an interval is allowed for quieting down the nerves of the officials; during this period of repose the latter have a little chat together while the wretched passengers employ their time in watching their unfinished repast being quietly consumed or cleared away by the waiters and hangers-on of the buffet.

Presently the Herr Oberschaffner having lighted a fresh cigar and told the last good thing to the station-master, who laughingly responds with one more telling still, instructs his subordinate to give the word "fertig" or "all right." Hereupon a man, who has been standing for some time by a bell under a handsome awning that forms a magnificent ornament to the platform, pulls the rope half a dozen times, winding up with a one, two, three, to intimate to all that this is really the very, very, very last time of sounding, and then finally a penny trumpet is sounded. As to the author of this last display of musical ability, there is some doubt, but in all probability it is due to the lungs of the Herr Oberschaffner. There remains now simply for the engine-driver to blow his whistle, and then, after a moment or two, as if time were necessary for the digestion of all this complicated

organization, the telegraph bells, which have
been incessantly performing a tinkle-inkle,
tinkle-inkle accompaniment, cease sounding,
and the train goes off in a leisurely manner,
quite befitting the philosophic and phlegmatic
character of the great nation whom it
serves.

To Niederdorf in the Pusterthal is a ride
by rail or carriage of three or four hours,
through scenery of great beauty, for at
times one has charming peeps of the silvery
peaks of the adjacent Dolomites. The
sights in the neighbourhood draw many
visitors to the valley, and the spas, for so
many of the larger villages are called,
are in the summer-time filled with strangers
from Vienna and North Italy.

This was the case on the arrival of the
Brotherhood, the "Höllenstein" hotel being
crowded to overflowing. It was past midnight, and the sleepy Boots who admitted

them seemed scarcely inclined to let them come in at all; it required both moral and physical persuasion in the end, and then the apartment proffered was one of very rough aspect, and contained already one occupant.

So uninviting indeed was the interior of the chamber, that it was some time before any one would venture inside to reconnoitre. At last White, with all the valour of a British Tittlebat, summoned courage to do so.

"Not a palatial residence," he said, groping cautiously forward.

"Very close and stuffy," said Green, sniffing about as he followed up.

Another moment and Brown was in the room. "Why, there's no ventilation at all," he said; "and there's one fellow already in possession."

Black timidly remained without, trying

to get a glimpse of the interior, and was commencing a protest with—" Oh, I say ; look here ; don't you know——" when the servant thought he had waited quite long enough, and so to assist the travellers in making up their minds, he fairly pushed the last man in and shut the door.

All eyes turned towards the man in possession, and some thoughts were entertained about provoking a quarrel, White suggesting, in a bloodthirsty manner, the advisability of pitching him out of window ; but as there was no window to pitch him out of, such a proceeding was out of the question, and the best had to be made of a bad job. The ordeal was, however, worth going through, if only for the purpose of becoming objects of commiseration next morning, and to receive the apologies of the people of the hotel when they found out how badly the poor Englishmen had been.

treated. There seems to have been some misgivings on the part of the landlady as soon as she heard the account from the porter, for early in the morning, when a servant brought up water for washing, the latter was instructed to search for information, and the sight, and especially the feel, of Green's plaid suit hanging up behind the door was sufficient to convince her of the high degree of the wearer. Accordingly the most profuse entreaties for pardon were made by the kind-hearted landlady and her pretty daughter, who, however, could not, throughout the whole day, forget the joke of four *vornehme Badegäste* having been cooped up all night in a lumber-room, with a peasant for companion. All charge for sleeping accommodation was foregone in the bill, although the full value of it was taken out in constant funny allusions by the *Kellnerinnen*.

An occasional wet day, which confines one in-doors, is sometimes not a disagreeable change, especially if you happen to be in an old-fashioned house. There is so much to look at in the antiquated ornaments about the room, so much to excite curiosity in the stained prints on the walls and the literature of the house. The *Fremden Buch*, or Visitors' Book, if an old one, is a fund of entertainment in itself, and in some cases, where the questions set down to be answered are strict and searching, there is some amusement too, for the straits to which conscientious travellers are put in replying to them are most comical. Thus in supplying information as to their destination, you find a traveller setting forth circumstantially that he intends going to Como and Maggiore, stopping by the way at Verona; while a thrifty sister, whose name is underneath, has subsequently

added, "if funds allow." One ingenious
Yankee, hailing from Philadelphia, had
brought with him gummed and printed
labels, giving the required information
about himself and family already set up,
and these were cleverly pasted into the
book whenever opportunity occurred. To
one of these grand labels some wag had
appended after the name the apt words,
" Printer, Philadelphia." It was the same,
probably, who specified his "travelling
documents" as ten-florin notes, and had
put down his ultimate "destination" as
" heaven."

Some of these *Fremden Bücher* are most
inquisitorial in their nature. Only fancy
being asked to give all sorts of news about
yourself for the mere purpose of gratifying
the gossiping *pensionnaires* of the hotel, who
pester the *Kellnerin* to take the book at once
to new arrivals as soon as they appear. By

way of example, here is an exact copy of the queries at the little village of Niederdorf, a quarter of an hour being required to fill in everything *en règle*. These are the headings of the columns :—

Angekommen sind am—(Arrived on the—).

Name und Zuname—(Name and Christian name.)

Character oder Beschäftigung oder Gewerbe der Ankommenden—(Rank, profession, or trade of the arrivals.)

Deren Alter—-(Their age.)

Religion—(Religion.)

Name und Zuname, Character oder Beschäftigung oder Gewerbe der Mitreisenden—(The name and Christian name, rank, profession, or trade of those accompanying the traveller.)

Familien und Dienerschaft—(Details of the family and servants.)

Deren Alter—(Their ages.)

Deren Zustand und Wohnort—(Their condition and native place.)

Woher die Reisenden gekommen sind—(Where the travellers have come from.)

Pass oder andere Reise Documente—(The nature of the tourist's passport or other travelling documents.)

Sind abgereist—(Destination and date of departure.)

Then besides the *Fremden Buch* there are the newspapers of the hotel to be studied, and of these the advertisements best repay perusal. The mixing up of business with social announcements is very quaint. Thus you may read an advertisement commencing :—

"Yesterday, died my dear wife," . . . . . and ending in "Depôt for all kinds of drugs."

After an announcement of birth comes a line at the bottom, "Good Dutch herrings."

But the most interesting met with was the following, which occurred in the pages of a Viennese paper, the *Constitutioneller Vorstadt Zeitung* ·—

"A substantial man of formed character, (widower), 32 years of age, of a very agreeable appearance (dark), having two pretty children (girls), of 5 and 3 years of age, in a good situation, possessing a capital of 1100 florins, with a good establishment, &c., desires as soon as possible to marry a substantial and domestically-educated maiden or widow, with a loving heart and a little property. Proposals to be addressed under the motto, 'Simple and pretty,' Poste Restante, Neubau."

Here is another advertisement, scarcely so romantic :—

"Machines for catching fleas. For ladies,

5 silbergroschens; for lapdogs, 2½ silber-groschens."

No one should go through the Puster-thal without visiting the Ampezzo valley, if only to get a peep at the pretty district around the Dolomites. All the way to Cortina the scenery is magnificent, one beautiful point being the entrance to the valley, as one looks up at the grey craggy portals that form the only inlet thereto.

CHAPTER XI.

BLITHELY enough does every one march now, after some three weeks' steady work. Straps have ceased to tighten of themselves, knapsacks sit more easily upon the back, and boots have left off being a source of annoyance. The mountain air blows freshly over the hill tops when starting away in the morning, and invigorates one's whole frame. Even the hot valleys are not to be despised if you will only start early enough, when the sun is yet low in the sky; for as you march along, with steep wooded slopes on either side, there, under the shadow of the big mountain walls, the coolness of night still lingers, and in the pure heart-thrilling atmosphere is an ether as intoxicating as nectar. The cold clear air in the pine woods sweeps softly against one's cheek, and the brow is freshened as with spray from a fountain.

No sense of fatigue now, and the gallant band have well earned exemption from it. The Marienburg and Plattenkogl they have stamped upon, the Pfandlscharte has been scaled, and even a spur of the Gross Glockner itself—the Berger Thörl—has been crossed. Simple marching over mountain roads must henceforth be regarded as mere child's play. There is no throwing off the knapsack to get a moment's respite, no mending of harness to delay the start whenever a halt is made. To sit down at the roadside, without so much as easing one's belts, is now the custom, or even to play a game of skittles in heavy marching order. And at

mid-day, when the usual rest is taken, each
does his duty quickly and cheerfully ; search
is made for a convenient stream in some
shady nook, and here, after a bath, a savoury
mess of soup is cooked. A model encamp-
ment is formed, and all rapidly fulfil their
various duties. Green has become an ad-
mirable cook, and is entrusted with all
general arrangements. He is exempt, by
right of his appointment, from serving in
the menial capacity of wood-collector or
fire-blower, and while others scramble off to
collect a faggot and find flat stones for a
hearth, the *chef* fills his can with water and
puts into it the right quantity of *Extractum
Carnis*, groats, or vermicelli. It is not until
the fire is fairly alight, and the mess almost
ready, that the subordinates are released
from work and permitted to take their bath.
Then after a few finishing touches to the
soup, luncheon is served. Each man con-

tributes what stale bread or biscuits he may have in his pockets, and a few slices of German sausage, with pepper and salt, and sometimes a mushroom having been added, all sit down to lunch. A wooden salad spoon forms a portion of each kit, and the toothsomeness of such a meal, served under these circumstances, surpasses that of calipash or calipee. After two or three hours' rest, a general wash up and cleaning of utensils follows; but as scullery assistants the Tittlebatonians do not shine, Brown being especially lazy and slovenly. To see the gallant leader scrubbing away at the soup tin at arm's length, or washing the greasy spoons down by the brook, is a finer sight even than to watch him in the capacity of laundress.

To Cortina is a day's walk of some five-and-twenty miles, and for those who prefer to ride, there is a diligence twice a

16

day from Niederdorf. The way may be much shortened if you leave the road after the first mile and go across country towards the Ampezzo valley. By entering the wood and ascending over the shoulder of the mountain, you get a wonderful view of the opening of the grand ravine. Before you stretches a magnificent ·panorama of sharp grey peaks, which stand out, like gigantic fangs, in bold relief against the blue sky and fleecy clouds. Through a gap in the wall or basin of rock the road passes, and by its side you can see the pretty Goblau lake sparkling in the sun —a beautiful turquoise gem fittingly set in the silvery grey crags around. Once fairly into the valley, you are surrounded by these mighty and jagged spires, which rise up in fantastic shapes from the black pine woods; and a little further on you come in sight of the far-famed Monte Cristall, standing alone in magnificent splendour, barring one's path in front. All the way there is a succession of grand and ever-changing scenes, now wild and gloomy, now supremely soft and pastoral.

But the Tittlebatonians have but time for a flying visit only to this charming nook, and soon they are back again at Nieder-dorf preparing to face homewards. Distances and days have to be reckoned with the greatest nicety, and there must now be no delay in bidding adieu to pleasant valleys, snowy peaks, shady woods, and foaming torrents; to the guitar, the zither, and the jodeling of the Tyrol, with its honest, friendly inhabitants.

To get to the Brenner line the Puster railway is again taken; that is to say, as soon as it can be got at; for the train when it approaches a station never can make up its mind to remain quiet at the

16—2

platform for a moment, but must needs go
moving eccentrically backwards and for-
wards for no apparent reason whatever;
and it is only after a great deal of signalling,
gesticulating, and shouting on the part of
the officials that the carriages are at last
brought to rest in the adjacent neighbourhood of the platform.   They have a capital
name for these slow trains in Germany—
that couple up and uncouple at every station, and saunter along at any rate they
choose—a name in frequent use, and yet
one scarcely capable of translation.   What
we understand by *Parliamentary,* and the
French by *Omnibus,* the Germans appro-
priately term *Bummelzug.*   The word is de-
rived from the verb *bummeln,* which meaneth
not so much to loaf about, as to stroll to
and fro without any fixed purpose.   Hans
Breitmann was a Bummler, or Bummer
rather; and the term is exceedingly well

exemplified by German students who may
be seen strolling for hours about a market
place, or in front of any little residential
palace that happens to be in their university
town. A Bummelzug therefore is a slow
slouching train, that goes on its journey in
a perfectly meaningless manner without any
definite, fixed purpose, and pulls up on the
slightest provocation for an indefinite period.
Let ever so small a Kellner at a big hotel
discover you intend starting by the Bummelzug in the morning, and he ceases to
have the slightest respect for you. Indeed,
he generally considers it his duty to warn
his chief—the Herr Oberkellner; and this
dignitary, without further ado, marches up
to you at once for an explanation. There
must surely be a misunderstanding, he
thinks; you cannot intend going by the
early train in the morning. Why, that is
merely a Bummelzug, he laughingly ex-

plains, and will not get to its destination
till some time after the Courierzug, or
Postzug, or Schnellzug, or by whatever
grand name it is called, arrives; besides,
nobody from *that* hotel ever went with the
much despised train.   And great indeed is
the Herr Oberkellner's disgust if he finds
you are not to be dissuaded from your purpose.   You will find it is the Boots, or
a stern military commissionaire, who brings
your bill next morning for payment.

But to return to the Pusterthal train, which
has by this time fairly come to a standstill.
The carriages are very full, and nowhere
is there room for the Great Britons.   They
are on the point of giving it up as a bad
job, when a very grimy but good-natured individual, in a blue blouse, beckons the party
to enter his compartment, clearing one-half
the carriage of some big baskets and
peasants that encumbered them.   In this way

the occupants are closely jammed up at
one end of the compartment, but that
is of no moment; there is now room for
the strangers to enter. Hereupon Brown
effects an entrance; but what is his astonishment and horror as he slowly and hesi-
tatingly ascends the steps, to find himself
grasped fervently by the hand, while a
group of delighted natives receive him as
an old friend. The three other travellers
are treated in like manner by the blue
blouse, the other provincials present openly
envying their companion his friendship
with such distinguished foreigners. However, the kind friend is good enough not
to carry pride too far, and is quite satisfied
now he has the Englishmen with him, and
can show off his grand acquaintances. He
sits smiling and laughing at Brown opposite; nodding pleasantly at that gentleman,
and asking now and then whether he said

anything. But as Brown will not take to
the proprietor of the blue garment, the
latter transfers his patronage to the others,
and winks knowingly at each one in turn
to show he remembers them all, and considers the whole proceeding an exquisite joke.
Whether it is that it suddenly occurs to
him that the Tittlebatonians have perhaps
forgotten all about him, or whether it is
for the sake of proving once more to the
other occupants of the carriage the footing
upon which he stands, is uncertain ; but
when, after repeated advances, he fails to
draw forth any remarks, he proceeds to
inquire of Brown how he slept the other
night at Niederdorf. The whole matter is
then explained, and in their dirty travelling
companion in the azure costume the Britons
recognise their recent bedfellow. And as
the spark of recognition bursts into flame
and illumines their countenances, it becomes

reflected in the faces of those around, who, one and all, testify their satisfaction that a countryman of theirs should have occupied so distinguished a position. Everything that can conduce to the comfort of the pedestrians is attended to; and the kindly peasants, at some inconvenience to themselves, keep for the rest of the journey densely packed at the end of the carriage, to allow their betters full and sufficient room. Brown and Black, nevertheless, can hardly be brought down from the summit of their dignity to recognise their whilom acquaintance; but both Green and White are delighted at the meeting, the latter noting down in his memo-book (to be imparted to Mrs. White on the first opportunity) the whole story, the moral to which, as he resolves to point out, bears out the maxims embodied in that tale so well known to all school lads, " The Good-natured Boy."

A more varied moving panorama than
that of the Puster valley as you move
along at the rate of five or ten miles an
hour is scarcely conceivable, the ever-
changing nature of the scene being truly
marvellous. Here you have a perfect sea
of foliage on either side, the billows of
waving branches reaching from hill to hill,
while a little further on there is nothing
to see but sharply edged crags, cold and
grey, standing in the midst of wild desolation. Anon you traverse the outlet of
some valley, whose glaciers of white crystals
are seen streaming down to the very edge
of verdant pasture land, and anon a homely
village is passed nestling by the side of a
trout stream, the ideal of peace and con-
tentment. As the valley of the Brenner is
neared the forests grow more extensive, and
you see nought upon the landscape but
undulating woodland, pines and beech re-

lieving any monotony that might be suggested.

At Franzensfeste, a fortress of stupendous
strength, which effectually guards the
narrow mouth of the important Brenner
pass, the outlet of the Puster valley is
reached, and here the traveller has a choice
of two routes, for he may turn north over
the pass to Munich, or go direct south to
Verona and Italy. The fortifications are upon
a most extensive scale, and on every side
embrasures command the points of the
compass, the Austrians setting great value
upon this military post, which will accom-
modate many thousand men. From the
fact that all the traffic passing south from
Central Europe goes over the Brenner, not
forgetting the Indian mail, the importance
of the station is at once manifest.

    *   *   *   *   *

There remains now but little to tell, for

the object of the Tittlebat Club being
accomplished, there is simply the journey
home to be recorded. The train is taken
south, through the grand Val Lagarina,
past Brixen and Bozen, and in half a dozen
hours one is in the middle of bright sparkling Verona. Who can fittingly describe
the bustling market-place of that genuine
Italian city, the grand old arena of red
marble, one of the most perfect in existence,
the quaint narrow streets, the antique city
gates, and the soft, musical cries of the
fruit vendors ? Who shall tell of the evening
promenades, the military bands, and the re-
freshing ices and cooling syrups that the gentlemen of Verona delight in? Who shall
speak of the sparkling black eyes, flashing
under veils and half screened by coquettish
fans, of the soft oval faces and olive com-
plexions, of the dainty tread and lofty carriage of the Veronese dames ? The white

bridal veil of Genoa and the bewitching angular headdress of South Italy are absent, it is true, but the costumes are none the less pretty for all that, and after the more solid and square features of South Germany, every other woman appears a beauty.

And now the journey is continued by railway due west, past the outlying redoubts of the strongest fortress of the Quadrilateral, and on until the hot plains are left behind and mountains again rise upon one's path. There come welcome peeps of the queenly Lago di Garda, whose soft outlines are veiled in azure mist, and whose placid waters look cool and inviting to the dusty traveller. On in the glaring heat and sunshine through a stretch of flat country, and then again past a succession of lovely scenes until the shores of Lake Lecco or Como are reached. A rest of a few hours succeeds, passed under the shady awning of a boat, propelled along lazily by a stalwart oarsman who stands in the scorching sun with little else but a big Panama hat to protect him, and who is cunning upon the subject of sly nooks and bays where a plunge into any depth of blue water may be had; so transparent is the limpid blue that the diver can scarcely believe himself in the element at all, until glancing upward, he sees above him a mirrored surface to which bubbles are rapidly rising. As he swims and toys with the water his eyes rest on the soft Italian landscape that sweeps gently down to the margin of the lake, whose azure tint outrivals that of the very sky above.

And then with the evening steamer on the lake of Como, past Varenna and Bellagio, to rest the night at Menaggio. A twilight stroll along the shore as far as Cadenabbia, whose bright villas are to be seen miles away, where merry groups of

visitors are heard, making the gardens echo
with laughter; back to bed, with the
stars shining above and the velvet outlines
of the mountains across the lake still
distinctly visible, and fireflies flitting
about, their tiny sparks twinkling as
they go.

A walk of eight miles brings Porlezza
into view on the shores of the Lugano Lake;
and until the steamer heaves in sight,
bound for the town of that name, the
Tittlebats put their knapsacks under
their heads and lie down to gaze upon the
smiling prospect in front. On one side the
mountains rise abruptly from the water's
edge, so that no road can pass along the
bank, the tiny villages and chalets built on
the slope being in danger of falling into the
blue waters, were they not attached like
fungi to the greenslopes. Drooping foliage
dips into the water, seeking to cool itself

therein, and trellised vines and leafy fig
trees cover the steep inclines. There is
something curious and immovable in the
water close to the shore that looks like a
man's hat, but it is so fixed and motionless
that it can hardly be so. Nevertheless it is
a human covering, for after a time it slowly
turns round and discovers its wearer reclin-
ing on the sandy beach immersed to the
neck. What is that that comes over the
placid water? Hark! there it is again. It
must be some one shouting from the white
canopied boat approaching the shore. The
truth is soon apparent. The Englishmen,
quietly as they have come and laid themselves down to rest, have been observed by
the lynx-eyed boatmen, and two of these
are now speeding up for a job. But hold;
this is an episode worth relating, and so a
pause must be made.

"Gentlemen   going   to   Lugano   by

steamer ?" asks one of the boatmen, as soon as the skiff touches land.

A nod in reply.

" We will row you there for the same money," continues the man.

" And get you in half an hour beforehand," adds the companion.

" But we travel second class," replied Brown, diplomatically in his best Italian, and still on his back.

The enterprise, under these circumstances, does not appear a very profitable one. As the Englishmen, however, seem to take but little interest in the matter, the sum of eight francs is ultimately suggested as the fare.

This is reasonable enough for two men and a boat to Lugano, so the bargain is struck, a clause being made in the agreement for a bath, en route, of half an hour's duration. Everything goes well, and the

17

men row with a will, the quiet motion of
the little bark being far more pleasant than
any noisy steamer. The men keep their
word as regards time, for within an hour
and a half there is the smooth-topped
Monte Salvatore standing out in front,
while to the right, nestling in a cosy
little bay and framed in clustering foliage,
is disclosed the little Swiss town of
Lugano.

But all this while the boat is not making
for the town, but a little way to the left,
and presently Brown asks why they do not
row to the pier.

"You stop at Lugano, do you not ?" says
the chief boatman.

"No," is the answer; "we must get a
carriage and go on to Maggiore at once, for
we shall try to reach Domo d'Ossola to-
night."

"Ah, well," says the man, "you will go

to the hotel, and, after a little dinner, you will be off again."

"No, certainly not," says Brown, curtly and decisively.

"Ah, well, then you will take horses and carriages at once, and have some dinner in the meantime; fine hotel, the Hôtel du Parc, good carriages, nice horses."

And this is why the boatmen are not rowing direct for the town. The kind-hearted fellows are resolved to take care of their passengers, and land them at an hotel of their own choosing; the boat is being rowed rapidly towards a neatly-built house on the quay, where, of course, paternal care will be exercised, and where perhaps the poor boatmen themselves will not be altogether forgotten. As far as the hotel is concerned it may probably be the best house in that part of the world, only it is the conveyance there willy-nilly,

17—2

the being paid-for-and-delivered-sort-of-
manner that causes a rising in the throat
of Britons, who never will be slaves.
The hotel is charmingly situated in front
of the lake; it has quite the air of a first-
class establishment, but the general aspect
seems somehow to whisper the item " service
and waxlights." There is, however, nothing
to lead one to believe that it is not unlike
all houses of *premier rang*, and one by one
the Tittlebats soften down and begin to
think that as matters are, perhaps they
may do worse than throw themselves upon
the mercy of the big hotel they are rapidly
approaching.

It begins to be tacitly decided upon to
enter the hostelry straightway, and bargain
for a carriage for continuing the journey.
But in an instant a circumstance occurs
which changes matters entirely, and brings
back the British feelings of obstinacy and

independence with twofold vigour. There is standing near the big portals a small urchin, and this far-seeing youth observing a boat-load of distinguished foreigners making direct for the hotel steps, jumps desperately at a big bell-handle over his head, and causes the most fearful din. The attention of all idlers within a wide radius is thus called to the circumstance, and these speed to the landing-place to look on, quite a little mob. But this is as nothing compared to the change that comes over the quiet and peaceful hotel. The effect is marvellous. If the reader has ever attended a performance at a circus or hippodrome, he will possibly remember the very first act of all. The circus, faultlessly raked, is empty, and silence reigns supreme; the curtain across the entrance to the ring is drawn, and nothing is seen of the performers, not so much as a stray groom

being visible; the orchestra has played
through the overture, and all is expectation
during the pause that ensues. Suddenly a
bell rings, the band bursts forth, the cur-
tains are drawn back, and there quickly
appear, stamping down the smoothly kept
tan in the circle, a dozen gentlemen in
tightly buttoned dress-coats, white waistcoats, and gold-laced trousers; and these
proceed to stand at attention on each side
of the door by which the splay-footed per-
former comes bounding in. Now if this
picture is borne in mind, the scene in front
of the hotel at Lugano can be easily imagined. For no sooner had the warning
been sounded by the urchin aforesaid, than
there issues forth, with quite a business,
circus-like air, a stout smiling gentleman in
a white waistcoat (no whip, however), a tall,
graceful individual in whiskers, evidently
the Herr Oberkellner, one or two minor

Kellners, and a commissionaire with a gold-
laced cap, while two minions of lower rank
in black calico-sleeves and green-baize aprons
descend the steps to receive the guests on
arrival. It is an impressive sight; and to
make the thing more effective the boatmen
redouble their energies, and putting on a
spurt, send the boat to the landing-place in
capital style. The effect is instantaneous;
grander travellers would have hesitated at
the moment, and the shoal of Tittlebats
are scared away off-hand; and instead of
the smug countenances of a minute ago,
the smiling would-be entertainers look upon
very blank faces, as one after another the
tourists are helped on land. They have
previously assumed their knapsacks, so there
are no loose packages to be seized upon,
and turning sharply to the right along the
quay they leave the group of gentlemen
in waiting free to follow their own devices.

With one of the many vetturinos hanging
about a bargain is struck for a carriage to
Luino, on the Lago Maggiore, and pending
its arrival the surly Britons sit in line upon
the parapet, their untidy boots dangling
against the granite wall, and their eyes
fixed upon the numerous retinue still
grouped around the big hotel; within a
quarter of an hour they are driving away
in time to catch the afternoon boat to Pallanza.

Along the Lago Maggiore, with its soft
low bank and pretty islands, to Pallanza,
where a conveyance is hired for Domo
d'Ossola, reached an hour after midnight.
Thence next day, a cool, cloudy day fortunately, across the grand Simplon Pass on
foot, a severe day's march, but as it is the last
walk of the tour and every one is in excellent
training, nothing is to be feared from a

little over-exertion. From Brieg, by early
diligence, to Sierre to get the morning train
to the Lake of Geneva, along a few dozen
miles of isolated railway which was projected
years ago as a " Route aux Indes," and
which has been more than once inaugurated
by brilliant international fêtes and orations.
When the whole length of line to India
will be complete it is difficult to say at present, but the last section of nine miles from
Sion to Sierre over a dead level, necessitated
a period of half a dozen years, the exertion
proving so great that an interval of exhaus-
tion has now set in, leaving matters in
abeyance. But the simple-minded inhabitants of the Rhone valley are still sanguine
of seeing the time when the whole vast trade
with India, bales of merchandize, rich
fabrics, spices and coffees, the shawls of the
luxurious East and other costly wares, will

be carried past their mountain villages. Meanwhile there is a very remunerative traffic being carried on with tourists, and in summer time the crowded state of the little stations of Sierre, Martigny, and St. Moritz, gives one the idea of a perpetual fair being held in the neighbourhood.

Thus to the shores of the Lake of Geneva, whence a boat possessed of all the qualities of its prototype the *Bummelzug*, having spent half a dozen hours in zigzagging across the broad blue water, at last makes up its mind to finish the business and make for Geneva. The good ship *Simplon* having once ventured close to the tourist-fleecing city, is quickly drawn into the vortex by the rushing Rhone, so boat and cargo glide quietly between the two curiously-shaped breakwaters, which appear to the traveller something like the upper and lower jaws of a shark.

And Geneva, as everybody knows, is now-a-days as near London as York was fifty years ago, when the fastest coach took four-and-twenty hours to travel the distance.

THE END.